"Your fath **clear that the last thing he wants is for his precious princess of a daughter to be with someone like me. So we are going to present him with that reality, Annie."**

She gasped.

"You and I will get married. It will be fast, it will be public, and it will be completely in his face. *I* will be in his face, and you, my dear Annie, if you want my help, will love me slavishly and devotedly in front of your father, lavishing me with affection, attention, until he almost can't stand it."

The world seemed to be cracking apart, splintering into a thousand pieces. It was too cruel, too impossible to contemplate.

"I can't believe you," she ground out. "How can you even suggest—"

Theo dropped her hand then, and the ice that seemed to flood her veins was a deluge of frigidity.

"This is nonnegotiable. They are the only terms that will allow me to contemplate breaking my usual practices and buying less than half of a stake in a company."

Clare Connelly was raised in small-town Australia among a family of avid readers. She spent much of her childhood up a tree, Harlequin book in hand. Clare is married to her own real-life hero, and they live in a bungalow near the sea with their two children. She is frequently found staring into space—a surefire sign she is in the world of her characters. She has a penchant for French food and ice-cold champagne, and Harlequin novels continue to be her favorite-ever books. Writing for Harlequin Presents is a long-held dream. Clare can be contacted via clareconnelly.com or on her Facebook page.

Books by Clare Connelly

Harlequin Presents

Pregnant Before the Proposal
Unwanted Royal Wife
Billion-Dollar Secret Between Them

Brooding Billionaire Brothers

The Sicilian's Deal for "I Do"
Contracted and Claimed by the Boss

The Diamond Club

His Runaway Royal

Royally Tempted

Twins for His Majesty

A Greek Inheritance Game

Billion-Dollar Dating Deception
Tycoon's Terms of Engagement

Visit the Author Profile page
at Harlequin.com for more titles.

BLACKMAIL
TO WHITE VEIL

CLARE CONNELLY

PRESENTS

MIX
Paper | Supporting responsible forestry
FSC® C021394
www.fsc.org

Harlequin® PRESENTS™

ISBN-13: 978-1-335-21361-7

Blackmail to White Veil

Harlequin Enterprises ULC
22 Adelaide St. West, 41st Floor
Toronto, Ontario M5H 4E3, Canada
www.Harlequin.com

HarperCollins Publishers
Macken House, 39/40 Mayor Street Upper,
Dublin 1, D01 C9W8, Ireland
www.HarperCollins.com

Printed in Lithuania

BLACKMAIL
TO WHITE VEIL

The Love Shack Ladies. It's often said that writing is a solitary endeavour, but with friends like you, it definitely doesn't feel like it! What a joy it is to be able to share this wonderful, exhilarating and at times frustrating journey with you.

PROLOGUE

THE HUNGER IN his belly was not a new sensation. He'd known it, on and off, for almost every one of his thirteen years. It was the kind of hunger that gnawed at a person from the inside out, so extreme one couldn't even faint from it, because the agony of being so utterly empty and depleted refused to allow any reprieve.

From where Theo sat, back pressed to the wall of an Athens street, he watched some of Europe's wealthiest and most elite pass him by, none so much as glancing at the grimy, skin-and-bones boy huddled on the ground—as though he were invisible. His clothes were tattered, his skin covered in soot and his eyes were sunken.

But oh, those dark grey eyes. They could still see. And his mind, though malnourished, could understand.

The inequities of this world. The imbalance. The unfairness.

He watched Europe's elite, as they moved like a relentless tide, undulating in and out of the revolving glass doors of one of Athens's most exclusive hotels, and inwardly, he cursed them all. How could there be such wealth in the world, when he had to live like this?

Still, it was better, in Theodoros Leonidas's opinion, than the alternative. He'd known many temporary homes, and had hated each and every one. It wasn't always the fault of the foster parents with whom he was placed. Theo appreciated that he was difficult—he'd been told it often enough, but he recognised the truth of it. He was angry and defensive, and given the choice between being thrown into the home of a stranger, or living on the streets with his own wits, he would always choose the latter.

Even when it meant a hunger such as this.

He closed his eyes. Not to sleep—his hunger wouldn't allow it—but to wait, and blot the world from his mind. As night fell, he would move, driven to take what no one would give him. Just a little food, to keep him going. Just a little food, for a young teenager with no one else to get it for him.

CHAPTER ONE

THE MAN ANNIE LANGLEY had known five years earlier wouldn't have been seen dead in a place like this, yet there he sat, in a booth on the other side of the exclusive Sydney bar—a regular haunt for him, apparently, while he was overseeing his Australian business interests. Once upon a time, Theo had *hated* this sort of place, had despised restaurants of its ilk, too. Back then, when they'd been young and purportedly 'in love', his idea of a good time had been sharing take-out at his apartment. Annie had known her over-protective parents wouldn't want her to get involved with someone like Theo—older, and more experienced, who'd lived rough. Keeping things low-key meant they weren't ever photographed, or spotted by high-society friends, and their relationship could remain a secret, so avoiding this sort of place had suited her, too.

A lot had changed in five years, though.

A familiar tide of grief surged through Annie, at what she'd lost and how she changed, but she forced herself to remain numb to it. Not to think about her mother's death, her father's slide into depression and grief and Annie's inability to hold it all together, no matter how hard she tried. Those might be the reasons for her having flown halfway around the world, from her home in Athens, to

Australia, to come face-to-face with the man she'd once imagined spending the rest of her life with.

The man she'd broken up with, and refused to speak to ever again.

Annie stood just inside the door, concealed by the plush burgundy curtains at the entry and the dozens of well-moneyed guests who stood between them, needing a moment—a lifetime?—to catch her breath and rebuild her courage.

This was a last resort—and it was a moment for last resorts, after all. Without help, her family's company would have to declare bankruptcy, and everything her parents had worked towards their whole lives would be destroyed. On Annie's watch.

Her throat thickened with the threat of tears, but she swallowed the. It was a time for strength and determination: not grief. Not fear. Not sadness—even when there was so very much to be sad about.

Digging her fingernails into her palms, Annie tried to focus on the Theo she'd fallen in love with. Not the Theo she'd crushed on from afar, when he'd first moved in next door. Then, she'd been just a girl of eleven, and the first time she'd spied him getting into his foster parents' car, across the expansive front lawns their properties shared, her heart had gone into total meltdown. From that point on, she'd achieved almost stalker-level obsession, the kind of adoration teenagers almost held a patent on.

She'd watched from afar, equal parts craving and fearing interactions, because having to talk to him left her tongue-tied. For the first time in her life, she'd cared about something and someone other than her parents and being the perfect daughter for them. Theo had started to take up a huge portion of her waking thoughts and sleeping dreams.

That seemed like ancient history now, though. Because eventually, he'd noticed her, too. When she was much, much older, on the night of her twenty-first birthday, and she'd begged him to kiss her, to make her teenage wishes come true… It had been the start of a whirlwind year, in which she'd sworn her heart had become so full it was at risk of bursting. For the first time in Annie's life, she felt seen for who she was, not what she was meant to represent, and it was all because of Theo.

That Theo had promised Annie he'd always be there for her, that if she ever needed anything, he would be her helpline. Her port in the storm.

That was the Theo she was appealing to for help, tonight. Not the Theo who'd been so coldly angry with her when she'd ended their relationship. Not the Theo who'd said such awful things, tearing her apart, piece by piece, and with such ease, until she was shaking and frozen to the core.

She couldn't think about that morning without wanting to slip into a crack in the earth's mantle and disappear for ever.

With knees that knocked together, she began to walk, slowly, carefully, through the crowd, wiping a trembling hand over the silky material of her champagne-coloured dress.

She'd grown up in this world, and had always been a part of it. Her parents' wealth had opened many doors for her, and the fact she'd gone to a prestigious international school meant her friendships had all been with children of similar financial backgrounds. Yet she'd never really felt at home in this sort of environment; it was like play-acting. Being the woman everyone expected her to be.

Except with Theo, a little voice reminded her, and out of nowhere, she was bombarded by memories of them together. Her in jeans and shirts, or better—his shirts, lounging around together like they had no money and no cares in the world. Watching silly action movies, ordering fast food, just being together. More than that, he'd let her be herself. Unlike her parents, who had seemed to exist purely to keep her alive at all costs. He'd loved taking her out on adventurous dates, like jetskiing or hiking or riding on his motorbike. Her parents would have had a conniption if they'd found out.

Palms moist with sweat, she was almost at his table when his eyes, slowly scanning the room, landed on her, and the whole entire world seemed to grind, loudly and tangibly, to a halt. The earth stood still, the dust from the tectonic plates' arresting flooding her throat and making everything dry. Legs that weren't quite steady were far better than this: legs that refused to cooperate. All she could do, was stand still too.

She stared at him through the veils of time, the man she'd just been thinking about—the man he'd been five years earlier—morphing into this version of him. Not visibly older, but somehow, so much harder. His face, which she supposed had always had a tightness to it, now radiated tension and cynicism. His eyes, which once upon a time she might have described as a dark grey, seemed almost black tonight, and as she looked at him, one corner of his lips lifted in a gesture that was far more mockery than smile.

With effort, she forced her legs to move, one after the other, carrying her the rest of the way across the room, until she was at the edge of his booth, hips pressed lightly to the table's edge for support. He had been wearing a suit, but the jacket was now discarded on the plush velvet seat to his side, and if there'd been a tie as well, it wasn't in evidence. Instead, his button-down shirt was undone at the collar to reveal the thick column of his tanned throat, and a hint of his chest; the sleeves were pushed up to just beneath his elbows, reminding her of how strong and leanly muscled his whole body was.

She glanced away quickly, drawing in a quick breath.

'My, my, if it isn't Annie Langley,' he drawled, that accent so familiar it panged in her belly. If he was surprised to see her, there was no evidence of it on his handsome symmetrical features. 'And here I thought I was rid of you for ever.'

It was like a knife being plunged into her heart anew. Their breakup had been…awful. Actually, that word was completely insufficient, but in the moment, Annie couldn't think of an alternative. The bleakest and most necessary decision of her life had led to an argument that still shook her insides if she thought of it.

'Nice to see you, too, Theo,' she managed to croak, her voice barely audible above the fashionable electronic music pulsing through the bar.

'I did not say it was nice,' he corrected, eyes on hers, probing her, so she squared her shoulders, refusing to let him see that she was intimidated or afraid.

'True. Do you have a minute?'

His lips flattened and for a moment, she thought he was going to say no. She hadn't let herself imagine that possibility, even when she'd known it was there. She hadn't wanted to contemplate what she'd do if he turned her away without giving her a chance to present her case to him.

'I'm meeting someone,' he said, glancing at his gold wristwatch.

'Okay, well, until they get here,' Annie said, desperately, and because she really couldn't take no for an answer, she slid into the booth opposite, immediately regretting it when their knees brushed beneath the table, and her pulse went into dangerous territory. Suddenly, she was twenty-one again, the young woman who'd loved and wanted with every fibre of her awakening body, and never had the chance to have.

His lips quirked in something like a mocking half smile, as he lifted a hand and immediately drew the attention of a waitress in a silky white blouse and fitted black pants.

'I'll have another.' He nodded towards his scotch. 'And something for the lady.' Even the way he said 'lady' was inflected with the kind of disdain that made her heart hurt.

'Of course, sir. What would you like, ma'am?'

Annie was about to refuse, but suddenly, the offer of some Dutch courage was infinitely tempting. 'Um, a white wine, please.'

'A sav?'

'Sure.' She nodded quickly, frankly not caring.

Theo said the name of a wine bottle, and the waitress beamed a megawatt smile his way. 'Oh, excellent choice.'

Annie resisted the impulse to roll her eyes. She needed Theo's help and she sure as heck wasn't going to get it by antagonising him. Out of nervous habit, she pulled her long, silky dark hair over one shoulder, the curls she'd carefully wrapped into it bouncing against her pale skin as she then toyed with her fingers in her lap, oblivious to the way his eyes were resting on her face, making their own inventory of changes.

'So, Annie,' he prompted, his voice a dry drawl. 'Is it a coincidence that you are here?'

'No,' she said. She had no intention of lying to him. 'I've been trying to contact you. Have you been getting my messages?'

Another twist of those lips that had once driven her wild with pleasure and promises. 'Yes, I've gotten them.'

Her heart trembled and the betrayal of that admission thudded against the walls of her gut. 'Oh, right.'

'You might remember, I asked you never to contact me again?'

'I remember,' she whispered, then cleared her throat. 'But I also remember you saying you'd always be there for me.'

For the briefest, tiniest moment, she thought his eyes showed something. A softening. Interest, remorse, concern? But it was gone so quickly, she realised she was layering her own wishful thinking over his expressions.

'That was a long time ago.'

'Not so long,' she said, as the waitress returned with a tray and two drinks. She cleared Theo's glass before replacing it, then slid Annie's wine to her. Annie wrapped her fingers around the stem gratefully, without lifting it to her lips.

'A lifetime.'

'Six years. Not even.'

He arched a single brow. 'Did you come here to discuss the past?'

Her lips parted on a quick sigh. 'No,' she said, dropping her gaze. There was no point. They'd said everything there was to say. She'd dumped him because her parents had insisted on it. He'd been angry at her reasoning, had fought for her to try to make it work, had fought for their relationship, and she'd shut him down. Again and again. It had not been an amicable split.

She took a quick sip of her drink, barely noticing the world-class wine as it spread across her palate.

'Then what is it? As I said, I'm waiting for someone, and it would be better if you weren't here when she arrives.'

She.

Annie ignored the rolling in her gut.

She knew he'd dated since they broke up. *Everyone* knew he'd dated. One of the richest men in the world, responsible for several tech innovations, as well as world-famous property developments, from Sydney to Dubai to Shanghai and Paris, Theodoros Leonidas had taken his foster parents' not-insignificant wealth and somehow turned it into a global powerhouse.

No, not somehow. She knew how he'd done it.

Because as often as there were pictures of him printed in the papers with beautiful women on his arm, there were stories written about him in the financial broadsheets: his ruthless, dog-eat-dog, take no prisoners negotiation style credited with his ability to make some of the toughest deals, and to walk away from anything that didn't serve him.

So what if he was waiting for a woman? That had

nothing to do with Annie. She wasn't here for personal reasons, but rather, for business.

'I have a proposition for you,' she said, a little unevenly, glugging back some more wine.

'I see,' he murmured, though his voice was now as cynical as his half smile had been earlier. 'How fascinating. And here I thought I had nothing to offer you.'

She flinched. 'It's better if we leave the past in the past.'

He dipped his head once, in what she took to be an agreement to that.

She took one more sip for courage. 'I'm here with an investment opportunity,' she said, faltering slightly.

His expression was sheer mockery now. 'Because you think I need help in that department?'

He could not make it any clearer how he felt about her if he grabbed a permanent marker and scrawled across the table, 'Annie Langley is Scum'.

Did she deserve that? Maybe. Every accusation he'd levelled at her in their break-up argument had been fair, and she understood the things he hadn't said. She'd chosen her parents over him, and to someone like Theo, that had been a betrayal. One he couldn't forgive. But he'd also misunderstood her reasoning. He'd thought it was because she was a snob, that her parents were snobs. He'd thought it was because he had grown up poor, that he didn't belong in their world. While that might have been true for some of Annie's friends, money had nothing to do with her parents' reactions. Not really. At its heart had just been their overarching need to keep her safe, and alive. Like they'd failed to do, from their perspective, for her older sister, Mary.

'And I'm here because you're the only person I know who can help.'

'Which is it, Annie? Charity or opportunity?'

She'd at least hoped he'd express a little concern when she told him it was about help, but there was that same icy tone in his voice.

'Both, I suppose.'

'Fascinating. Why don't you start at the beginning? You have precisely as long as it takes for my date to arrive so if I were you, I would not sit there fumbling with your hands longer than is necessary.'

She felt like the gauche teenager lusting after him that she'd once been. She swallowed, glancing away, his cruelty cutting her in a way she hadn't expected. Her eyes came to land on the wall just behind his shoulder.

'I'm looking for someone to buy a forty-five per cent stake in my parents' company,' she said.

She wasn't looking at him, so did not see the way he reacted to that, the tension that tautened his whole expression, the way his eyes darkened to almost black. Annie couldn't bring herself to see what she thought might be triumph in his face as she admitted, 'It's not in good shape, but there is so much scope for improvement and growth. You'd be getting a relative bargain and we'd...' *be able to keep going.*

The infusion of cash was just what she needed. And the addition of someone like Theo, to reassure their staff? They had been hemorrhaging leadership positions. The company was in an untenable position.

'I do not buy partial shares of companies,' he said, reaching for his scotch and taking a drink before replacing it on the tabletop. Her eyes slid to his and her heart twisted inside her chest.

'I know.' She swallowed. 'But I thought, in this in-stance—'

'That I would make an exception? And why, exactly would you think that, Annie?' He leaned forward a little way, bracing his elbows on the table, and she bit into her cheek, as she was reminded of just how big he was, how much larger than her. She'd always felt so safe, pressed to his side, or wrapped in his arms, like he was some kind of gladiator who could protect her from everything.

'Let me guess. Because, once upon a time, a long time ago, we went out, you think I owe you some kind of favour?'

She flinched again, visibly recoiling against his crude characterization of their relationship. 'We—did more than go out.'

His lip curled in that derisive way she'd seen several times already tonight. 'If you insist.'

She opened her mouth to argue, but then wondered if he was laying a trap for her. Getting her to go down memory lane and rehash their failed relationship, rather than stay on track and discuss her reason for being here.

'I've got all the financials for you,' she said, pull-ing a USB from her handbag and pressing it across the table. 'It's password-coded with your birthday.' Her voice hitched a little as she admitted the detail, but she'd wanted to protect the documents in case anything hap-pened to the USB, and hadn't wanted to use her own birthday, in case he didn't remember it, and had to admit that to her.

'Fascinating, but I told you, I do not buy partial stakes. That's not how I do business.'

'I'm aware of that. Did you think I'd come here to-night without doing my research?'

'Then you've wasted your time.'

'If you look at the details, you'll see it's still a good deal for you. What we can do in the market—'

'My date is here,' he said, moving from the booth, his jacket in one hand, his legs brushing hers beneath the table, so sparks flooded her bloodstream. He stood, un-folding to his full six and a half feet, his lap at her eye height, so she had to quickly wrench her gaze to his face. 'Excuse me, Annie. I'd say it was nice seeing you again, but we both know that would be a lie.'

He began to move away, to greet a woman who'd just walked in, wearing a denim mini skirt so short it al-most showed her bottom, and a camisole top with lace trim. Her hair was blond and glossy, and hung halfway down her back.

Annie watched as Theo's demeanour changed, his smile easy as he drew the woman into his arms and then kissed her on the lips. It was only brief, just a few sec-onds, but Annie acknowledged she could have lived her whole life quite happily without ever having to see that. It was bad enough that she'd seen photos of him with women clinging to his side like limpets, but those had been still photographs—a world of difference between that, and this.

Still, she'd come this far. She reached for the USB and curled it into her palm, crossing the bar and almost knocking a waitress off her feet in her haste to reach Theo and his date. They had already stepped outside by the time she caught up to them, and Annie, on auto-pilot, extended a hand to curve around his arm, to get his attention.

Theo glanced back at her, frowning, looking at her like he barely knew her now.

Hurt spread through Annie, but she refused to feel it. Later, when she was back in the hotel room, she'd wallow in the shame and degradation of this whole experience, but for now, she needed to make some headway.

'Just look at the financials,' was all she felt capable of saying, given the other woman was now staring at Annie, too. 'My phone number is in the document. I'm in Sydney for another two days. Take a look, and then call me.' She cleared her throat. 'Please, Theo.'

For a moment, his eyes narrowed, and then, without nodding, or uttering a word of reassurance, he took the USB from her and slid it into his pocket.

'Goodbye, Annie.'

She watched him walk away with no idea if she'd ever hear from him again.

CHAPTER TWO

THEO COULD HAVE gone a very long time without ever hearing the name Langley again. Annie had been one of the biggest miscalculations of his existence—and Theo didn't generally make mistakes, particularly not with people, and certainly not with trust.

Yet, he *had* trusted her. She'd worked her way through his carefully maintained defenses, wearing him down with persistence, and her insistence that she wasn't what he thought. So he'd let her in, bit by bit.

When Annie had turned eighteen, she'd drunk too much champagne with her snobby friends and begged him to kiss her. It had been a dare, he'd later found out, from the redhead she was always with—Bianca someone or other. They'd thought it was funny, how much Annie moped about after him with her oversized crush—given that he was just a street kid who'd moved into a mansion next door and never really belonged. He was certainly not someone anyone in that clique thought good enough for Annie Langley.

He'd refused to touch her.

She was barely more than a kid, and he hadn't been interested in providing entertainment for her entitled social circle.

But at twenty-one, it had been different. She was older, more experienced, completely sober, and as far as he knew, begging him to kiss her was all her own idea. Her friends were nowhere to be seen. And by then, he was the heir apparent to the Georgiades's fortune—his foster parents, having no children of their own, and having been blown away by Theo's business aptitude, had signed everything over to him. He was his own man, making his way in the world.

So, he'd kissed her.

That should have been the end of it. Except, even then, there'd been something addictive about Annie Langley. Something dangerous, too, because she seemed like the kind of person who could make him want what he'd never wanted before: to be needed. Loved. To want to stick around.

Theo had more than an average amount of experience with women; only Annie hadn't been anything like the women he usually slept with. She was so innocent and artless in her reactions, so responsive and hungry for him. It was a miracle they hadn't slept together that night—even more so that they hadn't slept together at all. Waiting had seemed right, with Annie.

At first, he'd done everything in his power to control their relationship. He'd wanted to keep Annie boxed into a single partition of his life. He enjoyed spending time with her, but he wouldn't let her shift his focus. Already, he'd made sweeping changes to his foster parents' business model, revolutionising their core values, increasing their wealth. He owed it to the child he'd once been to continue working towards his business success.

Yet night by night, in ways he still didn't understand,

she pushed at the walls of the partition he tried to keep her contained in, so that while it still existed, it morphed into something so much larger than he'd ever intended. She became the first thing he thought of when he woke up, the person he went to call when he had a success.

And then, she'd ended it, because her parents had told her he wasn't good enough for Annie. The worst part of it was that he knew her parents thought that, because her father had told him. Had tried to buy him off to end the relationship; had told Theo that he was the kind of man Annie needed to steer clear of. Didn't Theo understand that Annie was aristocracy? She was destined for greatness, and Theo was certainly not that.

He could never forget that conversation. As a street kid, he'd been called a lot of things, but somehow, hearing them from Elliot Langley had cut him to the quick. Because deep down, he'd wanted the other man's acceptance. The more he came to care for Annie, the more he knew it would be essential to earn her parents' approval to keep her in his life.

'Do you think I would ever allow my daughter to become serious with a man like you?' He'd jabbed a finger in Theo's direction. 'You are scum, from the darkest slums of the street. The Georgiadeses might have been fooled by your business acumen, but what do I care for that? My daughter can trace her lineage back to William the Conqueror, and who the hell are you? Do you even know, boy? How dare you so much as look at her, much less touch her. Much less think you have any right to get serious about her. If you ever speak to Annie again, you'll be sorry.'

It had gone on, and on, in that vein, but Theo had

blocked most of it out by then. He'd focused on assuming a mask of non-concern, sneering with half of his lip— and his insolence only angered Elliot further, so in the end, he was all but threatening to call the police for the very fact that Theo had once upon a time lived rough.

Theo hadn't taken the threat seriously. What could Elliot Langley do to him, after all? By then, Theo had been worth an absolute fortune, and in dating Annie, he wasn't breaking any laws. It wasn't the threat that shocked him, so much as the tone of his voice. The entitlement of the man had chilled Theo's blood, reminding him of how often he'd felt ashamed of his life on the streets, when he would walk past those incredible hotels and have wealthy couples turn up their noses at the sight of him. He remembered one such person making a cruel remark about the way he smelled. Another threw a half-eaten sandwich at him, where he sat on the footpath. And everything Elliot Langley said, in that conversation, brought it all back, and made Theo realise: the Langleys were just as bad as those people had been.

But it was Annie's betrayal that had stung, worst of all. Annie's betrayal that had made him feel foolish and stupid for ever having believed she was different to the rest of those moneyed bastards. When the next morning she arrived and told him it was over—coldly determined— he'd known instantly what her reasoning was. She was dumping him because her father had found out about them and insisted upon it. And Annie hadn't had the strength of character to stand up for their relationship. Whatever promises she'd made, whatever he'd thought they'd shared, had just been a construct of his mind.

Annie wasn't what he'd believed: she was just as super-ficial and snobby as her parents.

He swore that was the last he'd ever see of her, no mat-ter what, and he'd stuck firm to that. He'd sold the Geor-giades's house, having no interest in returning there, lest he happen to run into Annie again—or her father. He'd put her from his mind, focusing everything on business, his success, and yes, on other women. Yet now, after a brief ten-minute conversation in an overcrowded bar, she was suddenly back, bursting through the partitions of his brain just as quickly as before, taking over his thoughts in a way he bitterly resented.

He glared at the sweeping views of Sydney Harbour afforded by his penthouse suite, before finally giving up on resisting. He stalked across to his laptop and stabbed in the USB drive. He had fully intended to throw it out, but whenever his hand curved around the plastic to do just that, he saw the anguish in her eyes, heard the plea in her voice, and he shoved it back into his pocket.

Fine.

So he'd take a look.

What harm was there in seeing what her family's busi-ness was about? Even when he knew one thing for abso-lute certain: he would never, in a billion years, for all the money in the world, get in bed with the enemy. And that's what the Langleys were, and always would be, to him.

Annie really hadn't expected to hear from him again. His face had been the definition of immutable, his eyes chilling, his jaw locked in an expression that might as well have been a verbalised rejection.

Yet the next afternoon, his assistant had reached out to

arrange a meeting. Annie could well have been knocked over with a feather, but she'd kept her voice as steady as possible as she'd agreed to the details.

Not in an office, as she'd expected, but in the penthouse apartment Theo was based out of while overseeing the crucial phase of development approvals and design for a high-rise in the CBD.

A keycard had been left for her at the front desk, so that she could access his private level of the hotel, and as the elevator whooshed Annie upwards, she barely had twelve seconds to contemplate what this meeting would involve, and to quell her nerves.

She kept her focus on the necessity of this though, and on the hope that his agreeing to meet was a positive sign. She doubted he'd have arranged a meeting just to hand back the USB.

Yet, with Theo, and the way he'd been the other night, the animosity that had sparked from him to her, she couldn't rightly say what she was expecting when the elevator opened to reveal a huge tiled foyer with only a single door in it. She moved towards it a little hesitantly, cleared her throat then lifted her hand to knock, before realising there was a doorbell. She pressed it once, then stepped back and waited, hands fidgeting at her sides.

She was just about to ring the doorbell again when the door was pulled inwards and Theo was revealed on the other side, dressed almost the same as the other night—in a suit that had been dressed down. This time he wore no shoes, as well.

She was glad she'd opted to buy herself a suit—she felt better seeing him again dressed like this: for business. The navy pants were wide-legged, teamed with spike heels, and she'd tucked a cream-coloured blouse into them before adding the tailored blazer. Her hair she'd pulled into a neat pony tail, to remove the temptation to toy with it as much as possible.

'Annie,' he said, with a slight nod. It was a slightly better greeting than the night before. He gestured with his hand for her to enter the penthouse and she hesitated for only a millisecond before forcing herself to move through the door, ignoring the hint of his masculine fragrance she caught as she passed him.

Inside, she was immediately hit by the stunning view of the harbour, first, with the world-famous opera house right in front of her, and then, inside the apartment, the luxury of the furnishings. Not a cent had been spared in creating the kind of home away from home that only the world's wealthiest could possibly afford.

'Not bad,' she said, lips pulling to the side, trying to remember the Theo she'd known who'd been so averse to obvious signs of wealth, who'd virtually equated extravagance with the gutter. She turned to face him, and her stomach twisted viscerally. 'I was surprised to hear from you.'

His features shifted, ever so slightly, in a sort of acknowledgement of that.

'I take it you looked at the financials?'

'I looked at them, yes.' He crossed the room, so he was standing toe to toe with her, his nostrils flaring as he looked into her face. 'The company is in a mess.'

She winced. 'I know.'

'What happened?'

She let out an uneven breath as she tried to work out how to explain it all—how her father had barely been able to function after his wife—Annie's mother's—death, and so Annie had done her best to step into the breach. She'd also been grieving though—she'd barely recovered from the blow of losing Theo, and then her mother had died. So she'd hired a temporary business manager to work with her, but it had all gone pear-shaped.

'It's my fault,' she said, slowly, heavily, the admission hurting to say. 'I thought I could handle it, but I messed up, and if I don't fix it, if I can't fix it...'

He didn't say anything, but she felt the force of his gaze on her face. She refused to cry in front of him, but she did sniff a little, to stave off the emotions that were rioting through her.

'Why did you think I would be interested in this?'

She made herself meet his eyes. 'Because you used to care for me, and I thought there might be some part of you that still does.'

A muscle jerked in the base of his jaw. 'You were mistaken.'

It felt like a blade was slicing through her midsection. She nodded slowly, but now, anger was usurping grief. 'Is that why you organised this meeting? To see my reaction when you told me that to my face? I never had you pegged as a sadist, Theo.' She waited a moment, to see if he would explain, apologise, say *anything* that would lessen her anger, but he just stared her down, face neutral. Annie made a sound of disapproval, then began to stalk towards the door, but Theo was right behind her, his hand curving around her wrist, bringing her to a stop.

'I did not arrange this meeting to insult you,' he said, crisp and calm. 'I was genuinely curious about your reasoning for seeking me out. After all, you have many friends who could help you with this.'

Annie's heart hurt. The truth was, she'd seen what her friends were really like in that god-awful year of intense grief, when Theo was gone, and her mother had died. There wasn't a single one of them she'd turn to in a crisis. Not after that. When Annie was no longer a source of lighthearted fun, she'd ceased to be someone they thought of at all.

If anything, the last five years had turned her into a recluse.

'You made the most sense.'

'No, that can't be it. I drive hard bargains. I'm renowned for it—I was, even back then. You must know that having seen your financials, I would offer you only what the actual value of the company is—and such an amount would be an insult to your father.'

She noted the fact he referred only to her father, confirming that he knew her mother had died. And hadn't reached out.

She'd been dead to him, like he'd said she would be.

And oh, how she'd needed him then. How she'd wanted him to kiss her and make her tattered heart better.

'I had hoped—' but it had been a stupid hope.

'I'm not a charity.'

She flinched. 'The company is in bad shape—I'm the first to admit it. But the potential—'

'Yes, there is potential,' he admitted. 'To be frank, there is potential that I doubt it has even occurred to your father to think about harnessing, but I can see it. And if the company were mine, I have no doubt I could reverse its course in eighteen months.'

She drew in a shallow breath. 'Aren't you tempted, to see what you can do? When was the last time you had a challenge like this?'

His lips quirked in an expression of wry amusement. 'Every investment I make is a challenge. I seek that out.'

'So seek this out,' she half begged.

'I told you, when I acquire an asset, it is in its entirety. That's just how I do business.'

'I can't do that,' she whispered. 'I know I need help, to turn things around, but this is my father's pride and joy. He's lost so much, Theo, please, I can't ask him to lose this, too.'

For a moment, Theo's eyes flexed with a dark tumble of feelings, so Annie felt like the floor had fundamentally shifted beneath her feet.

'How badly do you want my help, Annie?'

She blinked, something like hope flickering, albeit briefly, in her chest. 'I—need it,' she admitted, aware she was putting all her cards on the table. 'I'm begging you, in fact.'

'Excellent. Now that we've established my preferred bargaining position, let me explain what would make this deal worthwhile, and we can see just how desperate you are, hmm?'

The hope flickering in her chest extinguished as wariness stole through her instead.

'I hate your father, Annie. I want to be clear about that, from the start. Your goal is to help him, my goal is to hurt him. However, through this merger, we can both achieve our ends. You should be aware, though, what my intentions are, going in.'

Her lips parted in shock at the darkness of that admission. 'How can you say that?' she whispered.

'Your father is an elitist snob, the kind of man who sees suffering and turns up his nose to face the other way. He is a judgemental bastard I would happily never think of again, for my entire life.'

Annie's heart felt as though a mountain had been dropped on it. She blinked now, unable to step the moistness gathering behind her eyes. 'How can you say that?' she repeated.

'We both know how—and why—I feel as I do. What you are perhaps not aware of is the amount your father offered me to leave you alone, nor the conversation we had that night. Unlike you, I told him precisely where he could take his interference. Unlike you, I chose to stand by our relationship.'

Annie's lips parted on a rush of shock. 'What?'

'If I hate your father, it is because of the things he said to me that night, the way he acted. I have no doubt he has said similar things to you about me, often enough, to spare us both the need for a rehashing of the conversation. Suffice it to say, he is not someone I would be interested in helping, were it not also a means to achieving my own ends.'

Annie could have been blown over by a light breeze. She could hardly think straight. She'd had no idea her father had gone to Theo, no idea he'd offered to pay him off, to get him out of Annie's life. Though she shouldn't have been surprised: her parents would stop at nothing to control every aspect of Annie's life, but she hadn't thought them capable of that. What had her father said to Theo? The idea of Elliot Langley offering Theo money made her skin feel all clammy—like she was some kind of commodity—but she couldn't focus on that now. She'd come here with a single purpose, and she didn't intend to leave empty-handed. 'What exactly are your "ends"?' she asked, steeling herself for whatever his response would be.

Annie hadn't realised he was still holding her wrist, until he started to stroke his thumb over the soft skin there. She glanced down, surprised by the familiar sight of his hand on her flesh, and how much it made her insides glow with warmth.

'Your father made it abundantly clear that the last thing he wants is for his precious princess of a daughter to be with someone like me. So we are going to present him with that reality, Annie.'

She gasped.

'You and I will get married. It will be fast, it will be public, and it will be completely in his face. *I* will be in his face, and you, my dear Annie, if you want my help, will love me slavishly and devotedly in front of your father, lavishing me with affection, attention, until he almost can't stand it.'

The world seemed to be cracking apart, splintering into a thousand pieces. It was too cruel, too impossible to contemplate.

'I can't believe you,' she ground out. 'How can you even suggest—'

He dropped her hand then and the ice that seemed to flood her veins was a deluge of frigidity.

'This is non-negotiable. Those are the only terms that will allow me to contemplate breaking my usual practices and buying less than half of a stake of a company.'

She shook her head, lifting a hand to her lips.

'And I will not just buy it, Annie. I will make it a point of pride to turn your father's company into a jewel of my crown. It will be ten times more valuable than he's ever dreamed of. I can make that happen—but only if you marry me.'

'You are such a bastard. How can I have ever thought otherwise?'

His smile was laced with cruel amusement. 'I'm not sure. Everyone else seemed to have my measure.'

She looked beyond him, towards the white leather sofa, then crossed the room and sank down into it. He was right. Everyone had warned her that he was dark, and tortured, that he'd been through too much for her to ever really be compatible with him. They'd all said he was unpredictable, that he'd hurt her. But she hadn't believed it. She hadn't, for one second, thought he was capable of behaving like this.

'They were right about you,' she said, squeezing her eyes shut on a surge of nausea. For years, she'd felt guilty and remorseful for having ended it with Theo, for having ignored her own affection for him, her own instincts, in favour of her parents' wishes. And now she saw they'd been right. Her friends who'd warned her had been right.

Theo was the devil, and here she was, trying to make a deal with him.

'By the way,' he said, moving into the kitchen, his tone now careless. 'In case you are wondering, this marriage will be real, in every way.'

When she looked up, it was to find his eyes latched to hers.

'Yes, by that I mean we'll share a bed. If I'm going to go along with this, there has to be some inducement.'

Her heart stammered; her pulse trembled. Did he have any idea what he was suggesting? Innocent Annie, who'd never been with a man before, was being propositioned into a loveless marriage that was to include sex.

Her voice wobbled as she said, quickly, 'You're the one who suggested marriage.'

'As I said, an inducement.'

She flinched, hating him for speaking to her like that. When they'd dated, he'd been so patient, so careful with her. He hadn't wanted to rush her, to pressure her; even when she'd been desperate to sleep with him, he'd said there was no rush. She shuddered now, at the ease with which he was trying to pressure her into a marriage that would include casual sex. 'You are horrible.'

'Apparently.'

'I can't—'

'That is your prerogative. I also have a business Realtor I can put you in touch with, if you'd prefer to find a buyer on the open market. I will warn you, though, you are likely to struggle to find someone who'll consider the company in its current state. Bankruptcy is more likely. And if you're thinking I wouldn't enjoy that prospect, then you really are clinging to some romantic notion of the man you thought I was.'

The grief devouring her was overwhelming. How had she been so stupid and wrong about him? How had she misread him so completely?

Besides, she knew a business Realtor wouldn't get her anywhere. She'd consulted with one six months ago, when she'd realised how badly things had been mishandled. He'd advised her just as Theo had—though he'd chosen his words with a little more compassion than the man opposite.

'Why on earth would you want to marry me?'

'I told you.'

'Just to hurt my father?'

He dipped his head in silent recognition of that.

'I can't believe it.'

'Nonetheless, those are the facts. And one more thing, Annie.'

She hadn't thought he was capable of anything else, but then he surprised her. 'Every single cent of my profits will go to a charity of my choosing, that supports children like I used to be. Every cent. Your father will see the company he loves so much flowing to the hands of impoverished street kids.'

Annie's jaw parted. Well, that wasn't something she had any problems with. After all, she'd still own a controlling stake, and the profits from that would be used to support her father.

'As for the percentage,' Theo continued, pulling the rug out from under her once more, 'only a fool would agree to allow you to continue to hold the lion's share. I will buy a fifty-five per cent stake, but,' he held up a finger to silence her. 'On the day we divorce, I shall return the whole thing to you. One hundred per cent.'

Annie's brain hurt too much to fully understand what he was saying. She shook her head. 'What?'

'I am not interested in owning your company long-term. I will take it over, fix it up, make your father rich again, then walk away. But he will have to know two things,' Theo said, his nostrils flaring with the force of his emotions. 'It is because of me,' he tilted his jaw. 'And that you were mine, for as long as it suited me, and then I left you, on my own terms. If you can live with that, then you have a deal. Otherwise, I wish you well.'

CHAPTER THREE

HE HADN'T BEEN surprised she'd told him to go to hell and stormed out of the penthouse. He'd been deliberately harsh in his offer, hoping she'd refuse. It was his standard operating procedure: only offer what he'd be happy to have accepted. Those were the only terms under which he operated. He'd intentionally presented the deal in such a way that made it almost impossible for a woman like Annie to acquiesce to.

Almost.

But then again, she'd loved her parents so much she'd given Theo up without a second thought. She'd lived her whole life in their shadow, had been theirs to control and dictate to. So it was little surprise that his doorbell rang a few hours later, and a fierce-looking Annie stood on the other side, her eyes sparking with sheer, unadulterated hatred and distaste, reminding him, for a moment, of her father, who'd regarded him with just such a look of scathing contempt, several years earlier.

Back then, Theo had still been just softened enough by Annie and her influence on him to have started to hope that the older man might one day look at Theo like a son. He'd still had a hope, somewhere deep inside, that he had a value beyond what he could bring to a company. He'd had a hope that he was worth loving.

How stupid he'd been.

Still a damaged child, hurt and seeking to be repaired, instead of just accepting that some people couldn't be fixed, and that was okay.

'Twice in one day, how fortunate,' he drawled, stepping back in silent invitation, but Annie shook her head.

'I don't need to come in. This won't take long.' If her expression had been a mask of contempt, then her voice was utterly dripping with it.

He had to admire her. When she'd left this place a few hours earlier, she'd been obviously furious, but also, clearly reeling. Her petite, slender frame had been shaking like a kitten, her skin whiter than snow. Now she was all fire and flame, spitting fury at him. He much preferred that—he felt more comfortable staring down anger than he did looking at pain, and knowing himself to be the cause.

'I'll go along with your proposal, but I have a counter proposal to offer.'

His admiration increased, but he didn't convey so much as a hint of that. 'Perhaps you're misunderstanding your bargaining position, Annie. I hold all the cards. You need something from me, and I need nothing from you.'

'I understand my position just fine, and I also understand you now. You're lying when you say you don't need anything from me—you revealed your hand this afternoon.'

Something crept inside his gut, a feeling like surprise. No one had stood up to him for a very long time—and the fact that challenge was now coming from Annie was strangely appealing. Strangely attractive too, if he was honest. 'Oh, did I?'

'You want revenge. You want to hurt my father. Hell, I'm pretty sure you want to hurt me.' She tilted her chin with courage, though, holding his gaze, even when her eyes were burning with rage and disgust. 'And that's fine. If that's the means to the end I need here, I'll go along with your sick plan. It will be worth it.'

In the back of his mind, he was aware of how empty his response was to her agreement. Usually, a victory elicited a rare moment of joy for Theo, a feeling that he was completing his purpose, that he was fulfilling the one thing he was good at. But Annie's acceptance left him strangely hollowed out, almost as if he really had wanted her to walk away.

'However, I need more.'

'More—' his skepticism sounded totally relaxed '—than the small fortune it will take to acquire your father's business?'

'I want a guarantee of a settlement in our divorce.'

His gaze narrowed. 'I already told you, you'll get the company.'

'Yes, but it occurs to me that you could gleefully destroy the company—whilst being married to me, your apparently fawning wife—thus utterly destroying my father for good. Only a fool would take that risk with a man like you.'

Her words cut through him like acid might a flimsy piece of fabric. That she could think him capable of such a betrayal was no surprise—not after the way he'd spoken to her this afternoon. But if there was one thing

Theodoros Leonidas lived and died by, it was his code of honour. 'My word is my bond,' he said darkly.

'Yes, well, it's not enough to bond me to you. I want an ironclad prenup, with a divorce settlement that will make this whole charade worthwhile, regardless of what happens with the company.'

'So you will walk away with the company and what? A multimillion-dollar settlement?'

'No,' her smile was saccharine. 'If you are able to re-build the company to an agreed-upon commercial value within eighteen months—and I will not be married to you for a day longer than that, you understand?—I'll forego the divorce settlement. It's one or the other. Believe me, I don't want a cent of yours if I can avoid it. But if we're going to do this to my father, I need to know he'll at least be financially looked after for the rest of his life.'

It was an *excellent* suggestion by her. He had abso-lutely no intention of going back on the promise he'd made her that afternoon, nor on reneging on the terms of their agreement, but her precaution was protective and wise, and very, very canny. He was so focused on her negotiating abilities, he didn't notice that she made no reference to her own comfort, and the rest of her own life—it was all about her father.

'And you agree that from the moment we put this in motion, our relationship will become public. Very, very public?'

Her cheeks flashed with a hint of colour—infinitely preferable to the paleness he'd seen that afternoon. 'That's part of the deal, yes.'

'Fine.' He nodded curtly. 'I'll have the wedding contract drawn up. Now, would you like to shake hands, or is there another way we can seal the deal?'

She glared at him, then took a step forward, her eyes overflowing with challenge as she spoke coldly and with barely contained rage. 'Let's be clear about something. I hate and despise you with every fibre of my being. I am marrying you for one reason, and one reason only: to save this company. I will do whatever you ask, I will be whatever you want, but know this, Theo—you have ruined, forever, anything good I ever thought of you. Any warmth I ever felt for you, any idea I ever held of you as some wonderful, perfect man. You destroyed that. *You.* I came to you at my lowest ebb, needing your friendship, and instead, you blackmailed me into a deal for the sole purpose of hurting my father. You are the lowest of the low, and I have never been gladder that I listened to sense and walked away from you back then.'

Each word was delivered like a slap to his skin, spiked and laced with intent, so it took all of his strength to simply stand there and absorb her words with a mask of impassivity, like she wasn't shredding a part of him to pieces he hadn't even known still existed.

'My lawyers will be in touch tomorrow,' he said, simply, so she nodded, and walked back towards the lift.

He'd thought that was it, but once she'd stepped inside, and was staring at him fearlessly, she said, 'I'd say I'm looking forward to it, but we'd both know that would be a lie.'

Annie knew Theo's intention was to hurt her father, and he probably wanted to do that by somehow getting their photos in the papers, and surprising the older man with the relationship. Over Annie's dead body. Having been contacted by Theo's intimidating team of lawyers that morning and gone over the prenuptial agreement, and had her own lawyer then peruse the documents and approve them before signing, she now faced the reality of what she'd agreed to. But it would all be worth it.

Since her mother's death, she'd done everything she could to hold her father and his company together, but it had been too much. Too much loss and grief for one man to bear, and Annie hadn't really been in the right headspace either, to do what was necessary.

Well, that was an error she intended to fix, right now, starting with this marriage. But it would be her way, her terms. Theo would live to rue the day he thought he could bully her into marriage and not pay the price. A smile tickled the corner of her lips as she reached for her phone—she was almost looking forward to making his life a misery.

Gone was the compliant, adoring girl who'd worshipped at his feet like a puppy dog. Now she was a modern-day Boadicea, without the titian-red hair and with a few more clothes. He wanted revenge? Yeah, well, he wasn't the only one.

She pressed her father's name in her phone and waited for it to connect. When he answered, she felt a pang in the centre of her chest. He was only in his early sixties— still a young man—but life had knocked the wind from his sails, and he sounded at least twenty years older than his age when his voice, thin and frail, came down the phone line.

'Annie, darling? Is everything okay?'

She swallowed past the lump in her throat, hating that

he always worried about her. 'Yes, Daddy, everything's fine.' She slipped into the childhood name out of habit. Though she'd been raised in Greece—her parents had fled there in grief, after Mary's death, needing a fresh start and a place where nothing reminded them of their late daughter—she was English, like her parents, and so were her habits and mannerisms. 'I'm calling with good news,' she said, infusing her voice with a happiness she didn't feel.

'Oh?' She could tell he was trying to rally himself, to remember what it was like to be happy for someone. 'Yes?'

'I'm getting married.'

Silence. She could just imagine his lined face growing even more creased with concern.

'It's okay, Daddy. This is a good thing.'

A sound of surprise. She pictured him sinking into the sofa, staring out at the view of Athens he had always loved from their palatial lounge room.

'I didn't know—I've been so—busy—I didn't even realise you were dating.'

'It's all happened very quickly,' she murmured. 'In fact, it's someone from my past. Someone you once knew, too.'

'Oh? Not that nice Beauchamp boy?' Her father named one of the many young men her parents had set her up with over the years. All nice, all handsome, all left her utterly desolate and cold. Disinterested and bored.

'No, not Harry Beauchamp. You know we're just friends.'

A sound of disappointment. 'Randall Chesterton?'

'No, Dad. It's…' She hesitated a moment, aware that

her father would *not* be at all pleased but knowing she had to get this over with, like ripping off a plaster. 'It's Theo Leonidas. Remember, from next door?' she said, as though they hadn't had a screaming match over her parents' insistence that she break up with him. As though that awful, awful night wasn't etched in both their hearts.

'Leonidas?' he said, his voice no longer just weary, but worried, too. 'No, Annie. I told you, that boy is—'

'He's not a boy, Dad. He's a man, and he's the man I've chosen to marry. I need you to accept that, and be happy for me.' Her voice cracked a little, as a tear slid down her cheek, thudding against the carpet.

'I can't do that. He's wrong for you, all wrong.'

Her heart splintered. If only she could be honest with him—but that would hurt him more. She had to convince her father that she was happy and safe. Which was ironic, because that was also part of what Theo had insisted on. They were to fool her father into believing the marriage was real, and joyous. For Theo's part, he hoped that would wound Elliot Langley, and Annie knew it would. But there was still a part of her that hoped her father might find it within himself to have a normal parental reaction: happiness for the choice of his child. After all, she had been through enough in her life to know that she was making the right decision, given the cards she'd been dealt.

'You don't know him.'

'I know him,' her father contradicted swiftly. 'He is the last person your mother or I want in your life. Please, don't do this.'

She closed her eyes on a wave of frustration.

'We dealt with this,' her father pushed. 'You broke

up. You've dated other nice men. Men who are far more suitable for you.'

Yes, she'd broken up with Theo, but not without a fight. She had argued with them, she had fought for them to understand, to give him a chance, but then, her mother had suffered the first of a series of heart attacks, and what choice had Annie had?

But now the circumstances were different. She was fighting for their financial standing, and for the family company her father cherished—one of the few things he had left from the tatters of their family.

'We're going to get married quickly, Daddy. I was thinking a garden wedding, at home, something simple,' she said, then realised Theo had said it needed to be public. 'Though we've also talked about a hotel, in the city. The details don't matter. But we want to be together, for the rest of our lives.' The words stuck in her throat a little, because of how desperately she'd felt them, six years earlier. 'And we want that to start right away.'

'Oh, Annie. I cannot support this.'

'Whether you support it or not, it's happening.'

'But, Annie. Who is this man? You know nothing about his family, and you are—'

'I know, I know. You've told me how you feel about him, but that doesn't change anything.'

'I can't accept this.'

'I'm sorry to hurt you,' she whispered, with honesty. 'But it's just how it has to be.'

'Are you sure?'

Annie almost laughed in despair. Was she sure? Sure that this could backfire spectacularly, yes. Sure about anything else…debatable.

'I'm getting married, and I want you to be happy for me.'

'I will never be able to give you that,' was all he said, in reply, before disconnecting the call.

She'd extended her stay by a couple of nights in accordance with a handwritten note that had been dropped off with the prenuptial agreement, stating that Theo would pick her up for dinner the following night at eight o'clock. On the afternoon of their appointed 'date', or rather, the beginning of her 'sentence', as she'd started to think of it, a bag from a designer boutique was brought up by the hotel concierge, with another note in Theo's darkly confident handwriting.

'For tonight.'

She'd pulled the dress from the bag once back in her hotel room, and marvelled at the elegant simplicity of it. She had bought and worn enough expensive dresses in her life to know the brand was one of the most exclusive in the world. She couldn't resist trying it on, and the moment she glanced at her reflection in the mirror, she was very, very tempted to wear it. It transformed her into a sophisticated, elegant heiress—just the kind of woman everyone expected her to be. Everyone except Theo, she might have said, if this wasn't evidence to the contrary.

She slipped the dress off again before she could weaken, stuffing it back in the bag before choosing something far simpler from her wardrobe—a black cocktail dress that fell to just above her knees and hugged her body like a second skin. She styled her hair in a braid that ran like a crown around her head, and kept her make-up minimalistic. For jewelry, she chose only her mother's earrings—pearls, which reminded her so much of Elizabeth Langley it couldn't help but bring Annie a shot of strength to wear them.

Her door buzzed at eight o'clock—on the dot—and Annie's stomach suddenly burst to life with butterflies and a dragon's fiery flames. She was hot and cold as she crossed the far more modest hotel room to the door, and wrenched it inwards to find Theo on the other side, in yet another suit, though this time, with the sleeves down, jacket on, and custom shoes, no doubt, firmly in place.

He took one look at her and flattened his lips in a line of disapproval. Hardly a compliment, yet she dipped her head to hide a grin.

'You didn't like the dress?'

'I didn't need the dress,' she corrected, glancing up at him when she was confident her face once again bore a mask of casual non-concern.

'May I come in?' he said, though it was less of a question than a demand.

'I thought we were going out.'

'In good time.'

Her heart began to race faster at the thought of being alone with him in *her* hotel room, which, though elegant, was far more like an ordinary room in proportions. With one big king-sized bed in the middle.

He strode in and took a look around, frowning with bemusement to see she didn't have a suite.

'I only intended to stay here two nights,' she found herself saying defensively, as she shut the door. 'And I don't need more space than this.'

She'd taken two steps away from the door when the buzzer sounded and she paced back to it, opening it with a half smile in place. A waiter stood there with a room service trolley adorned with an ice bucket, French champagne, two flutes and chocolate-dipped strawberries.

'Ma'am,' he said politely. 'Would you like me to place this inside?'

Annie was too flummoxed to respond, but Theo's voice came down the narrow corridor. 'Leave the trolley, thank you.'

'Very good,' the waiter said, brandishing a small clipboard for Annie to sign.

She reached for it, but Theo was there, signing his own name with a flourish after adding a generous tip to the line on the bottom. The waiter disappeared down the corridor, leaving Theo to roll the trolley into a room that already felt far too small for them.

His eyes rested sardonically on Annie as he removed the champagne bottle and unfurled the foil top, then with a bang removed the cork.

'Are we celebrating?' she asked, one brow arched.

'I believe it's tradition to toast an engagement with champagne.'

'But ours is not a normal engagement. Behind closed doors, we don't need to pretend.'

'We can still toast to fresh starts.'

'Are you forgetting what I said the other day?' she demanded, nonetheless taking the glass he held out, hating the way her traitorous body responded to the feeling as her fingertips brushed his.

'Definitely not.'

'Good.'

'Are you afraid that you might forget, Annie?'

She almost spluttered at such a preposterous idea, and

took a big drink just to wash away the angry response she was tempted to deliver. 'I'm confident I won't,' she managed, a moment later.

One corner of his mouth shifted in a half grin.

'To the future,' he said.

'To us both getting what we want and never seeing each other again.'

'Eighteen months is a long time to wait for that.'

'It'll be worth it.'

He sipped his drink, eyes resting on her face. 'You love your father a great deal.'

'What kind of statement is that? He's my father—of course I love him.'

Theo's eyes flashed with something, and his response was unnerving. 'Do you think it's mutual?'

'I know it is,' she said, shuddering a little, because her parents' love had been overwhelming—to the point of stultifying. She'd only really acknowledged that after her mother passed away, and to Annie's shame, mixed in with her grief had been a sense of…freedom. Because her father had been so wrapped up in his own immense sadness, and Annie had, for the first time in her life, been able to make choices for herself, without her parents constantly worrying and watching.

Theo, though, was silent, and that bothered her. 'What would you know about love, anyway?' she muttered, sipping her drink.

'Not a thing,' he responded without hesitation, yet the answer left her cold. It reminded her of the conversational no-go zone that his childhood had always been.

She knew the basics. He'd been bounced between foster homes, had run away multiple times, and finally ended up with the Georgiadeses next door. But how he'd come to be with the childless older couple, had always been a mystery. Though Annie and Theo dated for a year, he had been carefully guarded with biographical details, always brushing her off with a half answer, or occasionally giving just enough information to satisfy her without really telling her anything. Yet something in the way he answered so readily now made a flick of sympathy stir in the pit of her belly.

The Georgiadeses loved him, she knew that, but she hoped that before them, there'd been at least someone. Everyone—even Theo—deserved love.

The silence in the room was like a form of static electricity, buzzing and humming, creating a sense of cotton wool filling her ears. Finally she spoke, just to cut through the tension. 'I spoke to my father this afternoon. I told him about us.'

Theo's eyes landed on hers. 'And?'

'Would you like me to tell you he bawled his eyes out? Begged me not to marry you?'

Theo's brow lifted. 'Did he?'

'I wouldn't say he's jumping over the moon about it, but he accepts it's happening. I think.'

His eyes gave nothing away. 'And the contracts?'

'With the lawyers.'

'I presume your father has to sign for the company?'

'The company passed to me legally on my twenty-fifth birthday. That was always their plan.'

Theo frowned. 'Yet you still refer to it as "your father's".'

'It's always been his. I never wanted it, truth be told.'

He nodded. 'No, you were going to own an art gallery, if I remember.'

She ignored the warmth that spread through her at his recollection of that small fact. She'd gone on and on about her dreams back then, and he wasn't stupid. Naturally he remembered.

'Just a childish fantasy.' She waved it away like it was meaningless.

'It didn't have to be. You could have opened the gallery at any point.'

'No, I couldn't.'

'Why not? You had money, time…'

She sipped her champagne and turned away from him, walking towards the bed and sinking down onto the edge of it, staring at the small kitchenette opposite rather than looking at Theo. She didn't want to explain any of this to him. To tell him what her life had been like after he'd left and she'd been all alone. And then, with her mother's death, the new reality that had faced her. It had been such a difficult time, made all the harder for how much she wanted the one thing she couldn't have: Theo.

'I gave up on childish dreams,' she said, instead, her voice heavy even to her own ears.

'Good.' He walked towards Annie then, standing right in front of her, before pressing a finger lightly to her chin and tilting her face upwards to meet his gaze. 'Realism is a better outlook, Annie. There's less room for disappointment.'

She could almost believe the advice came from a place of kindness, but then, Theo wasn't kind, and he certainly wasn't kind to her. She flinched her face away from his touch, grinding her teeth, and was rewarded by a mocking smile.

A moment later, he reached into his pocket and removed a black velvet box. 'This is for you.'

He handed the box over with no fanfare, no romance, nothing. Not that she'd have expected anything from Theo along those lines *now*, but the Theo she'd once loved, or thought she'd loved—oh, how she'd fantasised about this moment a thousand times back then. She cracked the velvet lid open and pulled a face at the monstrosity inside.

This was a ring that screamed 'look at me', and it was the very last thing Annie would ever have chosen.

'And here I thought you hated elitism,' she murmured, pulling the giant diamond solitaire ring from its home and squinting at the brightness as the brilliant cut speared thousands of little light prisms across the room. 'I mean, I'm going to stun someone with this thing.'

'I thought it would be what you'd like,' he said, shrugging. 'Certainly what your father would want—an ostentatious show of "love", the kind of thing a "suitable" aristocratic fiancé might gift you.'

'Tacky and garish? How well you know me,' she said, sliding it onto her finger and trying to guess whether it was fifteen or twenty carats.

'At least no one will miss it,' he said, and she glanced up at him again.

'You're enjoying this.'

'Yes.' He didn't attempt to deny it, nor to hide his pleasure. 'But there are other things I'm going to enjoy far more about marrying you, Annie.'

And despite everything she knew she should feel,

a slick of moist heat, of delicious, desperate warmth, flooded her body, and a pulse began to throb between her legs, so she glanced away sharply and then quickly stood up, almost bumping straight into him.

Damn him for still being able to do this to her. Damn him for being the only man she'd ever felt anything like this for. How she hated him for that! Hate was good, though. Hatred and rage were excellent protective mechanisms, though Annie didn't stop to wonder why she should think she needed to protect herself. Once bitten, twice shy was her mantra—no way would she let Theo in again. Not now she knew what he was capable of.

CHAPTER FOUR

FOUR WEEKS PASSED in the blink of an eye, and before Annie knew it, the wedding day arrived. She hadn't seen her fiancé since their dinner date in Sydney. She hadn't needed to. Photos of them had gone up online even as they'd been eating a meal, pretending to have a wonderful time, thus meeting his requirement that their engagement be public and known. No doubt, Theo had had someone tip off the paparazzi. It just made Annie glad that she'd forewarned her father. Having lost her mother to a bad heart, she worried about the same with her father, despite the fact he was in excellent health.

Although Theo's remarks had hinted at him being attracted to Annie, he'd dropped her at her hotel without so much as a suggestion of joining her. And she'd been glad for that, too. Not that she would have minded rejecting him.

Annie had left all of the wedding planning to Theo—or someone he hired. Had it been a real wedding, she would undoubtedly have wanted to weigh in on every single decision, but given that he had blackmailed her into this, she figured he could take on the stress of planning.

The only thing she'd done for herself was select the wedding gown and bridesmaid dresses. For the latter, she'd chosen a pale yellow prom style, and for the former, an elegant off-white silk slip with a dropped back. She wore three fine gold chains that dangled at different heights down her spine. She looked like she was going to a fancy party, rather than a wedding, and though she had conceded to the wearing of her mother's veil, she refused to let it cover her face like a bridal innocent—she was going into this with her eyes wide open. No need to pretend otherwise. Her glossy dark hair had been styled into voluminous curls that hung around her face, and her fingers were painted a simple nude. On her feet, she wore black stilettos—a striking contrast to the dress— and her lips were painted a deep red. She revelled in bucking the traditional bride model. This wasn't a traditional wedding.

Perhaps on some level it was because she wanted to save the real bridal gown and look for one day, if and when she were to marry for real. After all, in eighteen months or less she'd be free of Theo, and one day, surely, she'd meet someone special. Someone she might love, who would love her back, like she'd once upon a time thought Theo did.

She'd chosen two school friends to act as bridesmaids, though she hadn't felt close to them for a long time. Theo had organised a large wedding, so what choice did she have? She hadn't asked who he was having as groomsmen; she hadn't wanted to show interest in his life.

'Are you ready, my love?' her father, misty-eyed, asked as he poked his head around the door to her room in the luxurious Athens hotel suite Theo had booked out for the bridal party.

Annie stared at her reflection, drawing in a deep breath. Was she ready?

Not really.

And yet, at the same time, she just wanted to get this over with. The sooner they were married, the sooner Theo's money would flow into the company, and they could start focusing on how to rebuild it. Instead of a honeymoon, they'd have a corporate merger. Relief twisted inside Annie, even as butterflies overtook every part of her body.

'Darling?'

She blinked her gaze sideways to where her father stood, a hint of concern on his handsome face.

'Yes.' She forced a bright smile. 'I'm ready. Let's go.'

'Annie.' Her father hesitated, though. 'If you have any doubts, you can back out.'

Annie's heart thumped.

'You say you're happy, that this is what you want, but you look as though you're on the way to the executioner.'

Damn it. She had been brooding. She forced a bright smile. 'I'm nervous—isn't that normal for a wedding?'

'Not my wedding,' her father said, shaking his head. 'Marrying your mother was the happiest day of my life. I would do it a thousand times over if I could.'

Emotions threatened to topple Annie's determination. She ran her fingers over her veil, thinking of her mother, drawing strength from her even when she wasn't there. This was necessary, and marrying Theo would be the answer to all their problems; she had to do it. 'I'm getting married.'

'But today, and to him? Why not wait awhile. Meet some other men. You've barely dated—'

'No, Dad. No. It's Theo, or no one.' That was true, though not for the reasons her father might have supposed.

'Your mother would have hated this,' he said, and with such sadness and disapproval in his tone that Annie's heart splintered apart. She didn't want to disappoint her father, but this was the only way she could save the business. She dropped her hand from the veil, hoping he was wrong, hoping that Elizabeth Langley would have understood.

'I hope not,' Annie said.

Her father just grunted, shook his head, so Annie said, 'Are you going to be able to walk me down the aisle? Because I'll go alone, if I need to.'

She could see her father was actually contemplating that, which gave a good insight into how much he was against the wedding.

'Come on, Dad,' she cajoled. 'It's just a quick ceremony, and then it will be all over.' Or just beginning, for Annie. But to her relief, her father put his hand on her forearm to lead her deeper into the suite.

When they stepped into the main room of the suite, Angela and Maria stopped talking and came to Annie, hugging her. It all felt so performative, though. Annie would never have chosen this for her real wedding day, but that didn't matter because this was just a performance.

It was part of what Theo required, and she'd go along with it, purely to get what she wanted: help with the business.

The wedding itself was to take place in the hotel ballroom. They rode down the lift as a group, and then walked through the corridor to a large set of double doors. Several staff members stood there in suits, and a woman with an earpiece and clipboard nodded her approval when Annie appeared.

'Right on time, excellent. Are you ready?'

Annie nodded.

'Good. Bridesmaids, here, and here.' She pointed to the carpet near the door, then turned back to Annie. 'I'll tell you when to go.'

Annie turned to her father, then slid her hand into the crook of his arm. He looked grey beneath his tan and a pang of remorse filtered through her. She'd do anything to spare him this pain, only it was the lesser of two evils. Allowing the company to become bankrupt would utterly destroy him. She couldn't do it.

The doors opened and there was a huge amount of noise as the assembled guests—goodness, there must have been four hundred people, at least—stood as one, like a tide rising, and turned to face the door. A familiar classical song filtered through to them, and then, Angela and Maria began to walk down the aisle. They obstructed Annie's view of Theo, so it wasn't until they were almost at the front of the assembled guests that she saw him, flanked on one side by two men in dark suits. But she barely looked at them, except to see if they were familiar—they weren't. Her eyes were trapped by Theo, locked to him in a way that made her whole body tingle.

He wore a jet black tuxedo, with his dark hair brushed back from his brow, and his face was hawk-like—studying her, perhaps wondering if she was going to bolt. Not likely.

She straightened her spine, squeezed her dad's hand,

and then, began to walk, slowly, as though she were enjoying it, down the aisle, even managing to shape her bright red lips into a curve, as though she were genuinely jubilant to be there. Wasn't that the point? To sell this as a love match?

But the closer they got to Theo, the more her heart started to ram against her ribs, the more her knees felt trembly and her pulse weak, so that by the time they came to him, she was barely aware of the way her father's body had grown tense and rigid.

'Elliot,' Theo said, voice gruff, eyes glinting with something that Annie knew to be triumph. He reached out and took Annie's hand from her father's, a symbol of his removing an object deeply valued, so she wanted to shake his touch off her—but she didn't. She was playing a role. She did, however, turn to her dad and kiss his cheek, and say, 'I love you, Daddy,' smiling at him encouragingly.

The older man's eyes slid to Theo's, and for a second, Annie wondered if he was going to say something. As far as she knew, this was the first time they'd come face-to-face since the conversation Theo had only recently enlightened her to having taken place, three or so years earlier. He didn't, though. A moment later, Elliot Langley turned and walked to his seat at the front of the audience.

Annie moved closer to Theo, and then, staring at him, her heart almost gave out, because this felt so close to what she'd fantasised about, so often, she couldn't believe it was happening—and like this.

He leaned closer to her, and murmured in her ear, 'You look beautiful.'

It was the last thing she'd expected him to say. Kind

and flattering—she hadn't thought him capable any longer.

'Thank you,' she whispered.

He pulled his head back, turned to the celebrant, and nodded.

'Dearly beloved…' Annie tried not to think about the wedding beyond being a scripted event. She didn't want to think about what would come next, about the night ahead, about the next eighteen months. She repeated the lines as required, smiled, and almost went into a form of stasis. But when Theo lifted her hand to slide the wedding ring in place, his touch was electric, shocking her out of the almost sedated state she'd fallen into.

And then, of course, came the kiss.

That part she'd prepared for, braced herself for. They'd kissed hundreds of times, so she knew what kissing him felt like.

At least, she thought she did.

But when this Theo swept her into his arms, holding her body tight against his, and dropped his head, the whole world began to spin way too fast. He smelled so good and felt so strong, his presence was overwhelming, right down to a cellular level. She simply parted her lips and then he was kissing her, his mouth not gentle, not brief, but rather, possessive and dominating, his lips parting her mouth wider, his tongue clashing with hers, his body shifting her slightly to shield them from the view of the audience, for the most part. It was not a long kiss— perhaps five seconds at most, but it was earth-shattering, regardless. When he lifted his head, she stared up at him, dazed, in a fog of need that he'd stirred so easily.

It was such a different kiss to before. Almost as

though back then he'd treated her like she was young and innocent. As though he hadn't wanted to break her, when now, Annie realised, she wanted that. She wanted rough and hard and flooded with passion—it felt appropriate, in their vitriolic new relationship.

'If there were not five hundred people staring at us, you would be naked by now,' he muttered, eyes dragging from hers to her mouth, to her breasts, which had peaked nipples and were flooded with tingling awareness.

'That's a little presumptuous, isn't it?' she said huskily.

His laugh was hoarse and mocking. 'No. Nice try, though.'

He shifted them so they were once more in full view of the assembled guests, and that was it. They were married.

After the wedding came the party, and though it was filled with loud revellers and good wishes, Annie knew barely anyone and found she didn't want to speak to many people. It surprised her that Theo had invited such a large number of guests. Then again, his business interests were enormous—he employed tens of thousands of people around the globe, so within those ranks, presumably he had large executive teams. No doubt they'd all received an invitation.

From what she could tell, none of the guests were particularly close friends with Theo. She watched him work the room though, the way he spoke to almost everyone, from what she could tell, his body language relaxed, his manner charming. She'd never seen this side of him before: she was surprised he possessed it. So debonair and sophisticated, you could easily imagine he'd been born to this sort of wealth and privilege. Perhaps that was the point.

She knew he guarded the truth of his upbringing with care; he probably preferred to interact with people who simply presumed he was every bit as entitled as they were.

At almost midnight, he circled back to Annie, who'd been having a mind-numbing conversation about child-care with two of her high school friends who were married with small children. They were debating the merits of their nannies, comparing the duties each performed, and Annie had to keep biting back a yawn.

'You look exhausted,' Theo murmured in her ear from behind, surprising her with his approach.

She startled, as his warm breath caressed her cheek. 'Thank you so much. That's just what every bride wants to hear on her wedding day.'

He shrugged insolently. 'It is a point of fact.' His eyes raked her face. 'Shall we?'

'Shall we what?'

'Leave.'

She looked around. 'Can we do that?'

'Yes, Annie. It's time.' And from the way his eyes held hers, she guessed there was a double meaning to his statement. Her stomach twisted in knots as he reached down and laced their fingers together, guiding her from the wedding ballroom, and out into the night.

'Honeymoon?' Annie repeated drowsily, as his car pulled up—not, as she'd expected, to his Athens home—but rather at a small private airport. She'd fallen asleep almost as soon as they'd left the hotel, and it was only Theo's words, 'it's time for our honeymoon', that had wakened her. 'But why?'

'Is it not what usually follows a wedding?'

'Yes, but this isn't a real wedding,' she said, as though she were talking to someone very dimwitted.

'Tsk, tsk,' he murmured, reaching over and unbuckling her seatbelt, then leaving his hand to hover on her hip a moment. 'Remember that we agreed it would be real, in every way?'

A shiver of anticipation brushed through her. 'Yes, but…'

'This is not up for negotiation. The arrangements have been made.' He pulled back and opened his car door, leaving her staring, frowning, at the black leather seat across from her. He then opened her car door, and stared down at her. 'I will carry you, Annie, if you do not walk yourself.'

She stared at him, half tempted to act belligerently and remain in the car, just to feel his big strong arms wrap around her again. But what kind of stupid was that? Where was the dignity?

She clamped her lips together and glared at him as she stepped out, shivering for a different reason now. Despite the warmth of the day, the night had turned cool, and her slip of a dress was hardly adequate protection.

Theo immediately slipped out of his tuxedo jacket and wrapped it around her shoulders. If she hadn't known for herself how unfeeling he was, she might have experienced a sense of warmth at his thoughtfulness.

'I'm fine,' she said dismissively, starting to shake out of it.

But his strong hands pressed to her shoulders, keeping the jacket in place. 'Wear it, Annie. It's not going to kill you.'

She made a noise of skepticism, but chose not to fight with him.

A private jet was just across from them, and going by the 'Leonidas' on the tail, it clearly belonged to Theo. It was not a small jet, either, but rather the size of a commercial airliner. Curiosity propelled her forward, then up the stairs, and when she reached the top and stepped inside her eyes almost popped out of her head. For there she was confronted with the most incredible space she'd ever seen. It was more six-star hotel than plane, from the plush lounge suite at the front, to a full dining table, an enormous flat screen TV on the back wall. She presumed there would be a bedroom and bathroom beyond that, and who knew what else?

'Jeez, Theo, this is…' She waved a hand in the air, searching for the right word.

He glanced from her to the plane, waiting without speaking.

'This is a lot.'

'Yes.'

She ran her hand over the back of one of the leather lounge chairs, moving deeper into the plane. 'Did you have this when we dated?'

'No.'

She nodded, wondering why he'd bought it, and when. She moved past the dining table, which she supposed he might use for boardroom meetings, and past more comfortable chairs that were angled to face the cinema screen. A partition with a timber-looking door was beyond the screen. She turned to face Theo, only to find he was almost on top of her, so when she stopped walking, his chest brushed against hers, and warmth licked her every cell.

'Can I keep going?'

His eyes flared again, in that way he had. A brief flicker of flame, of passion, before he could control it. Fascinating.

He dipped his head in acknowledgement, and Annie turned away again, glad for the reprieve of looking right at him. She opened the door, and stepped right into an enormous bedroom. It took up almost the whole back of the plane, with its king-sized bed, sofa and another huge screen.

Just looking at the bed made her mouth go dry. She twisted the enormous engagement ring on her finger, the huge diamond something she'd strangely gotten used to over the preceding four weeks despite her initial disdain for it. To distract herself from the bed, she pointed to two other doors. 'What's through there?'

'The gym,' he murmured, close enough that she could feel his breath on the top of her head. 'And the bathroom. There's time to freshen up and change before take-off, if you'd like.'

Her heart twisted at the simple courtesy. It had been a long day, and the thought of a hot shower and fresh clothes was suddenly instantly appealing.

'My bag?' she asked.

'Stowed, but there are clothes in there for you.'

'Oh.'

He really had thought of everything. Then again, it probably wasn't the first time he'd 'entertained' on his luxury plane. The thought drained the warmth from her body, leaving her ice-cold.

'I won't be long,' she said, turning from him easily now, and wrenching open the door to the en suite. As she might have come to expect, given the rest of the plane's fit-out, it was also the kind of room that would be more at home in a mansion than a plane, with white tiles, gold fittings and a shower that was big enough for two.

Yes, definitely a flying bachelor pad, she thought with distaste, as she slid the dress from her body, then her silky white briefs. The water came out warm and with good pressure, so she stepped under it and just stood there for several minutes, before reaching for the body wash and lathering herself all over, ignoring the way even her own touch sent sparks of need through her over-sensitised nervous system.

She hated that he could so easily do this to her, and yet...anticipation was a flickering flame in the pit of her stomach.

This marriage was a necessary evil, so far as Annie was concerned, except in one way. There was no deny-ing their physical connection, and even though Annie barely recognised the man he'd become—so filled with hate and rage—she knew better than to lie to herself.

She wanted him, just as much as she always had. It was a need that defied logic and explanation—it was simply a part of her.

Ten minutes later, she had dried herself off with a towel, and dressed in one of the outfits that had been left hanging in the wardrobe—a simple pair of shorts and a comfortable T-shirt. It hardly screamed seduction, but maybe that was a good defense to what they were inevitably hurtling towards.

She fidgeted her fingers and counted to ten before opening the door to the bedroom and scanning it for Theo, only he wasn't there. She frowned, padding through the plane in the towelling slippers she'd found, back into the main living area. Disappointment was a heavy stone in her gut.

She'd expected him to be in the bedroom. She'd wanted him to be there, waiting for her, and she couldn't believe that. What kind of fool did that make her? A lamb, willingly led to slaughter, that's what.

His eyes glanced up from the newspaper he was reading when she entered, and perhaps he saw the vestiges of disappointment on her features, because his smile was one of mocking indolence.

'Something the matter?'

'Of course not,' she snapped, taking the seat across the aisle from him. 'Where are we going, anyway?'

'My island.'

'Your *island*?' she repeated. 'Since when?'

'I've had it a long time, in fact.'

She frowned. 'You've never mentioned it before.'

'It never came up.'

She looked across the corridor towards him. 'That's weird, because it feels like something you probably should have mentioned.'

'Why, Annie? Do you think knowing I had an island might have convinced your friends and your parents that I was good enough for you, after all?'

She flinched at that anger in his voice, the barely concealed disgust.

CLARE CONNELLY 69

'No, I just think it's something that's not super common, and as such, wouldn't have killed you to tell me.'

'It never occurred to me to mention it. I bought it as an investment.'

She pulled a face. 'You bought an island as an investment?'

'The former owner got into financial difficulties, and needed to sell it quickly and quietly. I had the cash, so I bought it.'

'In cash.'

'Annie, you grew up surrounded by wealth, yet you seem totally baffled by the fact I have these things, like an island, and a private jet,' he said, gesturing to the plane. Before she could answer, a flight attendant in a smart grey suit strolled down the aisle, a tray balanced skillfully on one hand. She removed a flute of champagne, only half filled, and a mineral water, giving the latter to Theo and the former to Annie, before placing a tray of cheese and crackers in front of Annie.

'We'll be taking off shortly, sir,' she directed to Theo, then smiled at Annie before retreating. If she thought it strange that the newlyweds were sitting separated by an aisle, so what? Annie was tired of playing the part of the loving wife—it had been a long day and night, and she wanted to let the mask drop, just for a little while.

'You always hated status symbols,' she said, when they were alone again.

'This is not a status symbol, it's a practical necessity. I have operations all over the world. I travel frequently, often on short notice. I choose to do so in comfort and privacy.'

'And the island?'

'Is worth triple what I paid for it,' he said nonchalantly.

She shook her head, something still not adding up for Annie. Then again, how well had she really known Theo? Back then, she would have said she knew him better than she knew even herself, but it turned out, he was nothing like she thought.

'Do you go there often?'

'No.'

'So you have a private island—where exactly?'

'Off the coast of Italy.'

'Right, okay. So you have a private Mediterranean island, but you don't even use it?'

'What's your point?'

She couldn't say, exactly, only it sounded both sad and wasteful. 'Why don't you go there?'

'I don't have the time.'

She knitted her brows together. 'Because you work so much?'

'You sound skeptical.'

'No, I'm not, I always knew your work was important to you.' It was true. He'd acted like he had a monkey on his back, and building himself the biggest and best business empire in the world was the only way he'd ever shake it off.

His eyes glowed when they met hers, and she felt the fierce determination that was like iron in his veins.

'You have an active social life, though,' she said, as the engines began to roar to life and the plane accelerated along the tarmac.

His smile was laced with knowing cynicism. 'Social life, or sex life?'

Her stomach seemed to flood with acid. She glanced

away, her finger running up and down the slender stem of her champagne flute. 'I guess sex life, if you have to be crude about it.'

'And how would you know that, Annie?'

She jerked her gaze back to him, hating that he sounded so triumphant, like he'd caught her out in admitting she was basically his stalker.

'It's not hard to know it,' she snapped. 'You have a habit of going to high-profile bars and restaurants and you're incredibly rich, successful and handsome, so guess what? Your photo gets on all the social media gossip sites and in the tabloids. I can't so much as scroll Insta without seeing you and some vampy-looking woman on my feed. Tell me, Theo, is that what does it for you these days?'

'What, exactly?'

'Skirts that barely cover cheeks, boobs pretty much out on display. Is that your thing now?'

'How do you know it wasn't always my thing?'

That stung. Annie had simply worked on the assumption that *she* had been his ideal woman when they'd dated, but for all she knew, he'd been coveting something else all along. Wishing she was more sophisticated, that she'd dress like all her friends did.

'I really, really hate you,' she said, glancing towards the window and staring out, as the plane lifted up and Athens turned into a delicate blanket of lights, far beneath them.

'Be that as it may, you're married to me for the next eighteen months, and I find that's all I really care about.' She heard the snapping of his seatbelt. 'I'll be in the bedroom. If you feel like joining me, you're more than welcome.'

CHAPTER FIVE

THE FEELING OF satisfaction he'd been hoping for never came. Ever since she'd agreed to marry him, he'd expected that the wedding would ease the strange heaviness in his chest, but if anything, seeing her dressed like a bride had tugged at something deep in his gut. A memory he'd refused to examine since they'd parted ways.

There had been a time when he'd fantasised about this future with Annie, for real. A time when he'd not only imagined but simply accepted as fate a future life with her constantly by his side.

For someone like Theo, who'd been let down by everyone he'd ever known, who'd learned from a very young age that he was the only person he could rely on, the way she'd slipped into his life without his realising it, becoming a part of him without his consent, had been shocking.

Accepting their breakup had been a little like leaping off a tall building—he'd had to scrape himself up and rebuild himself, piece by piece, *without* her at the centre of his being.

And, he had done it. He had excised her from his thoughts with sheer strength of will, had cut her from his mind, and from his heart, where he had begun to understand she'd taken up the most shocking residence.

With time and perspective, he'd realised that caring for Annie had weakened him, and made him vulnerable, in a way he never intended to be again. Whereas life on the streets, his whole damned childhood, had made Theo tough, carved him like granite, something about Annie had eroded that. Or threatened to. He hadn't liked it—not once she'd ended things, and he'd realised how much of an impact she was having on him. He'd been relieved they were done, so he could go back to his solitary, diamond-tough existence.

And yet, he still did care. Not *for* her, in the same way he once idiotically had, but about her. Despite every shred of anger he felt for her snobby parents, and for the fact she'd so easily fallen into their plans, he hadn't enjoyed seeing her today. When she wouldn't notice, he had watched her. He had seen the tension in her features, the worry in her eyes as she'd sought out her father, to reassure herself he was okay.

This, though, had been a promise he'd made himself, that very morning they'd broken up.

Part of rebuilding himself had been knowing he would one day get his own revenge.

He had thought it would come just from his success. Her parents hadn't believed he was good enough for Annie? Then he would become the most successful, lusted-after man on earth, the kind of man ambitious parents would give their left arms to have their daughters marry. He'd spend a lifetime with women like Annie's friends between his sheets, and he'd make sure everyone saw that.

He would wave his success—and his womanising—in their faces. Yes, Annie's, too. He'd relished the thought of her seeing those photos. Every woman he went out with, and paparazzi snapped images of, he imagined her seeing and regretting the decision she'd made.

It had been a childish, stupid anger—totally beneath him—but there it was.

It would never have gone beyond making himself *this*, the very image of unquantifiable wealth and success, but for the fact Annie had turned up in his life and handed him revenge on a silver platter. How could he say no?

He'd acted on instincts, but now that they were actually legally married, he couldn't help wondering if he'd made a rare mistake. He'd acted on the assumption that he could easily control his feelings for Annie this time around—and that included the powerful desire that flared between them. But just a few minutes in her company had left his insides zinging—with physical need, yes, but with something else, too. A confusing array of uncertainty, and a lack of clarity when it came to his plan.

With frustration zipping through him, and a need to refocus on his goals here, he changed into shorts and a shirt and made his way into the gym. A run would help—or at least burn off some of the energy that had a stranglehold on his body and wouldn't let go.

Annie wanted, with all of herself, to go to the bedroom and get this over with. Not because she wasn't looking forward to it, but because she *was*. She wanted him so badly it almost hurt, and the thought of making love to Theo filled her with adrenalin. She hated that it was so, but there was no sense pretending otherwise, at least to herself.

The first time would be strange, though, because

everything was so different to back then, when she'd thought they were in love and going to spend the rest of their lives together. Then, she'd been desperate to sleep with him, to know the pleasure of his body, the togetherness of making love. It had been as much about their emotional connection as anything else, whereas now, it was sheer chemistry.

Just like their kiss at the wedding, when a different kind of passion had hummed between them. Something far more adult and overwhelming. Exhilarating, and exciting…she couldn't stop thinking about what it would be like to be with him now.

Yet, she stayed in her seat, stubbornly refusing to go back to the bedroom, even when he'd issued a lukewarm invitation for her to join him. Pride died a slow death, and Annie knew she would need to hold on to hers, in this marriage, which meant the only way they'd end up in bed together was if he pursued her.

She wasn't going to show him how much she wanted that, even when it was something she'd tacitly agreed to on the day he'd suggested this arrangement.

He didn't come back out to her until the plane was beginning its descent—and for Annie, that was a hair-raising enough experience as to leave her distracted by the perils of landing on an island in the middle of the sea to barely give him so much as a passing glance.

It was late at night, and the island was indistinguishable from the ocean—just a big patch of black that the plane was steadily careening towards. As they drew closer, however, she saw the runway lights guiding the pilots in to land, and in the distance, a gold glow which she presumed to be his house.

Curiosity then had her leaning forward in her seat to get a better view from the portal window, but she couldn't make out anything besides what looked to be a thickly lush amount of greenery on either side of the airstrip.

The plane touched down with a bump and she startled, glancing at Theo to see if he'd noticed, but he was once more absorbed in his newspaper.

She smothered a wry smile. So much for a honeymoon.

The house was definitely not what she'd expected. Oh, it was huge and modern and clearly very expensive, perched as it was right on the edge of the beach, with three walls being made almost solidly of glass. But it was the open plan nature of it that she hadn't expected. As in, no walls, except for the bathroom.

Despite being more than large enough to accommodate dozens of actual rooms, there were no partitioning walls. There was a massive kitchen and living area, with a grand piano and a flat screen TV the size of a cinema screen, several sitting areas, all plush and fashionably chic, and then, there was a bed. Just *one* bed. It was towards the back of the large room, but it was *right there* staring back at her, inviting her, demanding to be lain in and used for making love.

Heat flushed her cheeks as she dragged her gaze away to the blackness beyond the windows. In the morning, she would see the ocean in all its daytime glory, but for now, there was just a hint of silver foam, frothing atop the waves that rolled towards them, the cacophony of their crashing to the sandy shore rhythmic yet not at all reassuring. If anything, it formed a drumbeat of need, echoing the thundering of her pulse, making her want more than she wished to.

'This is it?' Her voice emerged squeaky and high-pitched. She swallowed, trying to tamp it down.

'Do you have a problem with it?' he asked, in a way that was almost completely blanked of emotion, and yet she heard it anyway—because she knew him too well to miss it. Smugness. He *wanted* to unsettle her. To make her uncomfortable.

She turned to face him, her eyes wide, but she shrugged, like it was no big deal. 'It'll do,' she said, moving through the room, running a hand over the shiny top of the grand piano, then pressing a few keys. 'Do you play?'

'No.'

She sat down on the stool and held her fingers to the keys, closing her eyes a moment before she began to move her fingers, to play Pachelbel's Canon in D, the song that she'd walked down the aisle to.

'I forgot you learned,' he said, his voice close by, so she opened her eyes to find him standing just in front of her, to the side of the piano, watching her with an intensity that made her blood fire. She ignored the insult buried in those words—the fact he'd forgotten she'd learned, when she couldn't forget anything about him.

Bastard.

'All my life,' she said. 'Well, until I was nineteen, anyway.'

'Why did you stop?'

'I guess I'd learned enough.'

'Do you still play for pleasure?'

Her lips twisted to the side. She hadn't played since

her mother had died. In the six months between her first and last heart attacks, she'd played for her often. Her mother had loved to hear Annie's music—it had reminded her of Mary. Mary, who'd been a brilliant pianist, who'd taught herself by the time she was three to play Mozart. Mary, who'd been a legitimate prodigy, and left Annie to follow after her, never as good, of course, no matter how much she practiced. That didn't matter, though. By the time she was proficient enough to play Mozart, her parents could close their eyes and pretend, for a little while.

'No,' she said, simply, when it was anything but.

'You are very good.'

She let the praise fall into a little black hole in her chest—a place that could never be filled, no matter what was said. She was competent, but she was not gifted, and her competence was really just a byproduct of how much she'd cared, how much she'd wanted to gift her parents her piano playing, as a token of love to Mary, and of their love for the daughter they'd lost.

'Why do you have the piano if you don't play?'

'It came with the house.'

'Ah.' She dropped her hands into her lap and looked around, then pulled her silky dark hair over one shoulder, toying with the ends distractedly as she considered the room. 'Was it all like this when you bought it?'

'Mostly.'

She bit into her lip—now washed clean of the burgundy lip stain and returned to their natural dusky pink. 'You didn't think about walls? Extra bedrooms?'

His eyes probed hers, and she felt the spark of heat

travel between them, felt it bloom in her belly then incinerate her whole soul.

'What for?'

'I don't know. Entertaining?'

'There are twelve bunks downstairs, for staff,' he said. 'If you're bothered by sharing a bed with your husband, you are welcome to use one of them.'

'Staff?' She clung to that. 'So, we're not completely alone here?'

His smirk showed that she'd given away too much of how she was feeling. Though it was very likely he'd mistaken her hesitation for a lack of willingness, when if anything, the opposite was true.

'The staff are for when I'm *not* here, which is most of the time. If I come to the island, it is to be alone. They leave me, then.'

'Just like that?' she pondered. 'You click your fingers and they simply disappear?'

'Believe it or not, they have lives and families off island that they're happy to return to.'

He was so confident within himself, so much a man now. Then again, he was when they were dating, too. His reputation in the boardroom had been forged from the time he turned eighteen and started stepping into his foster father's shoes, taking an already successful business and turning it into an empire. Seven years later, when they had started dating, he'd already made an enormous mark in the business world.

But with Annie, he'd just been… Theo. She'd always seen beyond his success, his achievements, to the man he was.

'I don't suppose you'd consider sleeping in a bunk

downstairs?' she asked, mainly because she felt like she *ought* to ask it. 'It would be the gentlemanly thing to do.'

He came to stand right in front of her then, pressing a finger to her chin and tilting her face to his, just like he had when he'd given her the engagement ring. 'We both know I'm not a gentleman though, don't we?'

Her heart turned over in her chest and it took every ounce of her willpower to deny that. A long time ago, she'd thought him the epitome of character and yes, gentlemanliness.

She swallowed past a bitterness in her throat as their eyes locked together in a battle of the wills. In a silent exchange, from which Annie had no idea if she, or he, emerged the victor. Eventually, he dropped his hand away, though remained close enough that if she shifted ever so slightly, her hand would be brushing against his leg.

'Are you afraid of me, Annie?'

The question surprised her, so too the delivery: deep and gruff.

She stared up at him, her eyes round, her pulse racing. She could tell him that of course she was—having seen the darkness in him, how could she not be? But the truth was, for some reason, she wasn't afraid. Not of Theo; she couldn't be. For as much as he clearly hated her father, and Annie, for what had happened five years ago, she still knew he'd never truly hurt her. Certainly not physically.

'No,' she answered, simply.

'Yet you're shaking all over.'

'Am I?' She hadn't noticed.

'Or is there another reason for you to be trembling

from head to toe?' he asked, and then his finger landed on her shoulder and stayed there a moment, hovering against the fabric of her T-shirt.

She shook her head, knowing why she was shaking, knowing he knew it, too. She hated her inexperience. Hated that he could stir her to this sort of fever pitch with just a look. If only she'd been with someone, then perhaps he wouldn't have this effect on her.

'That's a shame,' he murmured, letting his finger trail lower, to the upper part of her arm, and then flicking the shirt sleeve a little, so he could connect with her bare flesh. She had to bite back a groan.

'What is?' She couldn't think properly.

'That you're not willing to admit what you want.'

Her lips parted on a husky breath. 'Does it matter what I want?' she asked, trying to regain the upper hand. 'We both know what's going to happen. I'm as good as bought and paid for.'

His smile was laced with mockery. 'True,' he said, slowly. 'But I'm not interested in having sex with you on those terms.'

Her heart stammered. Something slipped inside of her. Doubts fired in her blood.

His finger tracked sideways, to the curve of her breast, and the nipple that was straining against the soft cotton of the shirt. He flicked it with his forefinger, his lips twisting at her obvious reaction—a gasp and then a soft, husky whimper.

'Are you saying—you don't want—' She couldn't finish the sentence. Not when he was now cupping her breast with possessive need.

'Oh, I want,' he ground out. 'Make no mistake about

it, I *need*. But what I wish for, most of all, is for you to beg for me,' he said. 'I want to hear you cry my name, as though you are driven almost mad with need for me.' He leaned closer, so his mouth was right by her ear. 'Only then will we both get the release we're craving.'

She whimpered, but before she could say anything else, his lips crashed to hers, just like in the wedding ceremony, hard and fast, possessive and desperate, and all semblance of thought fled from her mind, leaving only this. The immediacy and passion of their kiss, the white-hot desire that was exploding through her body. Her hands reached for him, even as his were tucking beneath her arms and lifting her, then pushing her back to sit on the keys, which clunked beneath her bottom. She pressed the ball of one foot to the piano stool as Theo stood between her legs, his lips expertly moving over hers, a masterclass in persuasion and temptation.

And though thought had deserted her, somewhere deep in the recesses of her brain was a strand of pride, whispering not to beg for him, not to give in to him. Not yet. Not so easily.

'You taste the same,' he said, into her mouth, and the words were discordant, initially making no sense. But after a moment, she realised he was talking about when they'd used to kiss, all those years ago.

'You're different,' she said, honestly, because he was. This Theo was all hard edges: in his behavior, his attitudes, his body, and his kiss. Everything was rough and harsh. Back then, he'd kissed her like he might break her. Now it was as though he was daring her to break him.

She scrunched her hand into the fabric of his shirt, her heart racing so hard she thought it might pound right out of her chest. The word *please* flooded her brain, screeching through her, but she buried it in their kiss, refusing to speak it, refusing to ask for him. Refusing to give him that satisfaction.

As if he could hear her determination, he pulled away from her, dark eyes glittering when they met hers. 'What do you want, Annie?'

Her pulse washed through her ears so loudly it was like a hurricane had come and whipped up the sea outside. She bit into her lip, refusing to say it, even when her body made a liar of her silence.

A single dark brow of Theo's lifted, and his expression was so calmly cynical that it was hard to know how *he* felt and what *he* wanted.

'Is this some kind of game to you?' she asked, after a beat.

He lifted a finger to her cheek, and stared at it, as if mesmerised. 'Everything is a game, in a way.'

'You don't seem like someone who's having much fun.'

'Don't I?'

She shivered. 'You're enjoying this?'

His eyes moved to hers and for a moment, she saw a glimpse of the man she'd once known, but it was gone again, immediately. 'I play to win,' he said, but it was too cryptic to understand. He straightened, his touch gone, her lips aching for his kiss, her body liquid with need. 'It's late. Go to sleep, Princess.' She flinched at his use of that name. He'd never called her that before, but her father did, and Theo knew it. She heard the disdain in his voice and a small, fragile part of her seemed to wither up and die.

CHAPTER SIX

ANNIE HAD FALLEN asleep in a state of utterly mixed and spent emotions. On the one hand, she'd been dreading Theo coming to bed, hating the thought of being so close and not touching him, hating the thought of wanting to reach for him, fearing that she might do so on autopilot. And yet, in the end, she'd been so utterly exhausted that she woke to the sound of crashing waves the next morning, in the exact same position she'd fallen asleep in—hugged right to the side of the bed.

Her eyes flared wide as she lay perfectly still and listened intently to see if she could hear Theo breathing beside her. Silence. Perhaps he had been a gentleman after all and slept on one of the huge couches?

She moved softly, flipping onto her back then turning her head to the pillow beside her. An indent showed he had lain there at some point, but when she brushed her hand over the sheets, they were cool to the touch.

With a small frown, she sat up, and took in the settings anew. The view now, in broad daylight, was beyond stunning. The glass windows showed a striking vista out over the ocean in one direction, unimpeded by anything, just beautiful sand and sea. It was the other windows though that displayed the landscape of the island like some kind of artwork—on one side, rugged, mountainous terrain, covered in lush greenery, and on the other, an expansive lawn, then colourful shrubs and trees, that made Annie itch to go out and explore.

The open-plan layout of the house meant that she could quickly ascertain that Theo wasn't here. Telling herself the fluttering in her stomach was relief, she pushed out of bed, the sunlight catching the enormous diamond on her ring finger as she moved the sheet aside, and paced towards the kitchen. She reached for a coffee pod, but stilled as she hooked a mug beneath the spout, her eyes arrested by something moving in the water.

Her mouth went dry as Theo drew his arms over his head, swimming in a horizontal line with the shore, each stroke powerful and contained, drawing him through the ancient waters as though it were butter and he a knife.

She struggled to properly inflate her lungs as she watched him swim, mesmerised both by his power, and the power of her memories. The first time they'd really kissed, in a way that had hinted at so much more, had been in his pool. Water lapping around them, his hands on her body, gentle but also promising, so she'd moved onto his lap where he sat on the pool step, straddling him, her own body answering that promise with one of her own. She'd felt him grow hard against her sex and a sharp throb of need had almost taken her breath away.

'Not now, Annie,' he'd murmured. 'Not yet.' Even when he'd wanted her, he had made sure she knew nothing would happen until she was ready. That she hadn't felt pressured or rushed.

She glanced away, tears filming her eyes unexpectedly, as the sweetness of that memory hit her for the discordancy with the situation they were in now—for the contrast between that Theo, to this. A man who told her she must beg for him before he'd give her what she wanted. Who wanted to belittle her, because five years ago, she'd had the hide to leave him.

She blinked quickly to clear the unwelcome tears, and finished making her coffee. Yet she stayed in the kitchen, eyes gravitating towards the sea, as he reached the far edge of the cove formed by the natural indentation of the island's shore, and turned around, to swim back the other way. His head lifted, just a sleek, dark shape in the bobbing ocean, but she took a step backwards, anyway, hiding from him, even when there was no way he'd be able to see her so quickly, and from so far away.

When he'd reached a space in the ocean that was in line with the house, he stopped swimming and stood, and her fingers went completely numb, so the coffee cup she'd been cradling slipped from her hands and smashed against the tiled floor. Her jaw dropped, and her eyes stayed glued to the visage of Theo emerging from the ocean, like some kind of ancient god, gloriously naked and absolutely masculine. They'd dated a long time, but she'd never seen him like this.

The closest she'd gotten had been when they'd swum together. This was a revelation and an awakening that sent her pulse skittering wildly.

She couldn't look away.

He was so bronzed and well-built, so muscled and strong, so lean and taut. Every step from the ocean was intentional and controlled, the rolling tide no match for this man. When he reached the water's edge, he paused, looking left and right, completely relaxed in his nudity, totally at one with the earth, the water, with himself. He continued to walk then, long, easy strides carrying him across the sand and closer to the house, so she swore, belatedly realising that he'd soon be there, with her. Naked? Her heart pounded as she galvanised herself into action, looking down at the black puddle of spilled coffee, and the shards of broken ceramic.

She stepped over it gingerly, towards the sink, opening the doors and finding paper towels. She was crouched down, mopping up the spill when the front door sounded.

She couldn't look.

She *couldn't*. Her cheeks flamed as she concentrated very, very hard on focusing on the job at hand and *not* thinking about the naked state she'd just observed.

'You're up,' he drawled, from close by, so she really had no option but to be brave and glance in his direction. She looked his way slowly though, as if steeling herself for what she might see.

Somehow, this was even harder than if he'd been naked. That she'd been prepared for. But a towel wrapped loosely around his hips, concealing his anatomy from her, but making her want to peel the towel away and take another peek, was all too confusing. She jerked her head back to the coffee cup quickly, but not so quickly she missed the quirk of his lips—a knowing smirk, as if he'd taken one look at her bright pink face and the spilled cup and worked out what was going on.

'Enjoy the view?'

Yes, that confirmed it, she thought ruefully. 'I've seen better,' she heard herself respond, the words curt—and untrue.

A hiss from between his teeth confirmed she'd hit her

mark. Well, good. His arrogance and the way he lorded her attraction to him over her was wearing thin. So what if she'd lusted after him from the minute she'd first laid eyes on him? That had been a schoolgirl crush, and it had prevented her from seeing him as he really was. It was only this last month in which the scales had fallen properly from her eyes.

'Are you trying to provoke me, Annie?'

'Why would I want to do that?'

'Perhaps you're trying to goad me into kissing you again.'

'Believe me, kissing you is the last thing I want to be doing,' she muttered, aware it was a dishonest statement to make.

He let out a sound of amusement, but then, to her chagrin, he was reaching down and pulling her to standing. They were so close, she could see the flecks of grey in his eyes, in amongst the dark, almost black. 'You are a liar,' he said, but it was with a hint of amusement.

'I'm not—'

He pressed a finger to her lips. 'We both know I could prove it, just by touching you.'

Embarrassment curdled in her gut, and she wished then, more than anything, that she'd at least slept with *someone*. It wasn't like she hadn't had opportunities. She'd been on dates, set up by her parents, and then later, after her mother had passed away, by her father. She knew she'd dated men who'd been attracted to her. But Annie had never felt a spark of interest in anyone besides this man, and back when they'd been an item, he'd been painfully determined not to rush her into bed.

'What's your point?' she asked, after a beat.

He dropped his finger lower, to her shoulder, his eyes shifting a little, before spearing her once more with the intensity of his gaze. 'I believe in calling a spade a spade. That's a quality I think we both share. You do not need to goad me into kissing you, Annie. I've already told you, ask for what you want, and I'll give it willingly.'

She swallowed past the lump in her throat. 'I can't work out if you want to demean me, by making me ask.'

His eyes flared wide.

'Is that it? Are you still so angry with me for daring to dump you, that your ego needs to be stroked by me now? Do you need to hear me say it was a mistake? That I wish we hadn't broken up?'

He swore then, a quiet yet guttural sound ripped from the depths of his belly.

'It was not a mistake,' he said, slowly, clearly. 'We both know that.'

The ground seemed to tilt beneath her feet. It was the last thing she'd expected him to say. 'Yes,' she said, valiantly, refusing to let him see that she was reeling. 'It was the right decision.' It had been. She couldn't have ever done anything to put her parents through more pain and grief. Even now, marrying Theo, whilst hurtful to her father, was simply the lesser of two evils.

'For a while, I thought I wanted something different with my life.' He was talking to her, but almost talking through her, as though he was back in the past, remembering the way he'd been then. 'But it was an illusion. *You* were an illusion.'

'I could say the same about you,' she muttered. 'The man I thought I was spending time with clearly doesn't exist.'

'That is also true. See how good we are at this honesty thing?'

'You want more honesty?' she asked.

'You've already told me you hate me,' he reminded her.

'I suppose it doesn't hurt to repeat it, though.'

'Nothing you say has the power to hurt me,' he said, simply. 'But you are welcome to keep trying.' He leaned closer, so his lips were just a hair's breadth from hers. 'I like fighting with you, Annie. I think we both know that if you keep it up, we'll end up in bed together, so by all means, do your worst.'

Her jaw dropped and her brain went blank. He was so casual about sex, about referring to going to bed together. Would he be the same if he knew she was a virgin?

Annie frowned, the idea not one she'd really contemplated. But somehow, she suspected even this version of Theo might balk at the idea of being her first lover under these circumstances. She was a twenty-seven-year-old innocent. Not really by choice or design, but because of circumstances. Almost her entire life, it had been about Theo. After their break-up, and her mother's death, she had come to the conclusion she didn't have a sexual bone in her body. She simply wasn't interested in dating, or exploring that side of herself.

'You have a one-track mind,' she muttered, and then he laughed, a deep, throaty sound.

'I take it back. Honesty is difficult for you.'

'Why do you say that?'

'If I were to touch you right now, you'd burst into flames. You are so hungry for me, you are practically drooling. Which is not to say I do not feel the same for you—but if I do have a one-track mind, it is something we share.'

Her tongue darted out, licking her lower lip. 'But we're not animals,' she said, her voice soft, though, most definitely lacking conviction.

'Actually, we are. And the desire we feel is the very definition of animalistic passion.'

Her cheeks flashed with warmth and her body felt unimaginably heavy. 'Well, you'd know more about that than I would.'

'Meaning?'

'That you're no stranger to casual sex, whereas I—'

'Only sleep with men your father approves of?' he supplied, a hint of anger in the words. She opened her mouth to dispute that, to throw her virginity in his face, but the words died in her throat.

She didn't want him to know. She didn't want to risk that it would change things between them.

'How does that work, Princess? Does he give you a list? Pre-screen your dates? Ask for proof of their aristocratic lineage before you're allowed to drop your pants?'

She closed her eyes, his questions stinging.

'I'd rather not talk about my father, particularly not with you, and definitely not now.'

'Why not now, *agape*?' He put his hands on her hips then, pulling her towards him, away from the spilled coffee and broken cup, and against the knot of his towel, beneath which she knew his dick was barely contained by the fabric.

Her tongue was thick in her mouth, and refusing to cooperate. She could barely think of words, much less say them. She felt backed into a corner, so all she could do was shake her head and feign exasperation. 'This is ridiculous,' she finally managed to squeeze out.

'Why?'

'Because I'm never going to beg you to make love to me. You're the one who said you wanted this to be a real marriage, you're the one who insisted on that. So if *you* want us to have sex, then fine. But don't expect me to take the first step.'

Another laugh, this one short and sharp, before he dropped his head so his lips were just an inch from hers and her pulse was a throbbing, twisty mess.

'Okay, I'll take the first step,' he said. 'Would you like me to kiss you?'

She rolled her eyes. 'You're still asking me to ask you.'

'I'm asking you to tell me,' he said. 'Tell me it's okay to kiss you.'

Her eyes widened, because it was a nuanced difference. He was asking for consent, for permission. She could say no, and he'd respect it. This was her line to draw. But a kiss was just a kiss. In fact, a kiss was a good way of showing him they could feel the stirrings of physical need and ignore them.

'I married you, didn't I?'

'That's not an answer.'

And despite having said she wouldn't take the first step, it was Annie who was lifting up onto the tips of her toes and seeking out his mouth with hers, Annie who was kissing Theo, Annie whose need was so strong she momentarily forgot everything they'd been, said, and were, and existed simply in the moment for *this*.

Annie kissed Theo, but she only had control for a few seconds before he was deepening the kiss and taking over, dominating her as he had at the piano, and earlier, at the wedding. It was Theo whose hands roamed her body, her back, her sides, before curving around her buttocks and pushing her forward, hard against him, against his arousal, his bare chest, Theo who ground his hips so she could feel *all* of him, so she moaned hungrily. Theo who made stars flood her eyes when he dragged his lips from her mouth to her jaw, flicking the pulse point there, before tracking upwards to the flesh just beneath her earlobe and sucking on it, the combination of his warm, moist mouth and his breath make her whimper and cry his name. Theo who lifted her and carried her to the bench, sitting her down and standing between her legs, kissing her until she was crying out. His name, a curse, but somehow, even in that moment, she was able to stop herself from begging for him, even when the word *please* ran around and around her mind like lightning in a bottle.

Last night, he'd cupped her breasts through her shirt but this morning, he had no patience for that, as he pushed the fabric up her stomach and over her head, removing the T-shirt carelessly, throwing it on the ground. She tilted her head backwards and his mouth dragged from her throat to her collarbone and then lower, his stubble rough against her soft skin, leaving pink marks in his wake, as he found a nipple and took it in his mouth, his hand squeezing her other nipple until the heat between her legs was a form of mind-altering madness, like some kind of hallucinogenic drug.

'Theo,' she groaned, and wiggled forward on the edge of the bench, needing to be closer to him, needing him. She wouldn't use her words to beg, but with her body, she pleaded, needing his touch, his possession, his everything.

'I want to hold your breasts when we make love,' he said, pulling up to look into her eyes. 'I want to take you from behind, and watch in the mirror as you fall apart.'

She shivered at the imagery, the heat of it, the promise, but she bit into her lip to stop herself from saying that she too wanted that. That she wanted everything he wanted. That she was utterly and completely in his hands.

'All that time, I stopped us from having sex,' he muttered, his hands now shifting to her thighs, one creeping higher, beneath the loose fabric of her shorts, all the way to where her leg met her body and resting there, before his fingers began to draw invisible circles, making her shiver. 'I didn't want to rush you, to pressure you. Yet now, all I can think about is the fact other men have had you, have worshipped you, and I have not. Do you have any idea how that feels?'

Intellectually she knew it was a gross double standard, given he'd lived whatever the opposite of celibacy was, but that didn't stop it from touching something deep inside of her. His jealousy. His possessiveness. Would he feel that if, on some level, he didn't care about her? Or was it all just about ego and ownership?

Before she could answer that, his hand had crept down a little, his finger finding her underpants and pushing them aside, then pressing against the heat of her sex.

His eyes latched to hers, a question in their depth, and he moved slowly. So slowly, as though he was giving her every opportunity to object, to tell him to stop. But she didn't. While she wasn't ever going to beg him— pride was on the line, after all—nor would she put a stop to *anything* they were doing, because it all felt too damned good.

It was Theo who moaned as he pushed a finger into her wet, warm core, brushing against the muscular wall so that Annie bucked her hips in pleasure.

'You are so wet,' he ground out, shaking his head a little. 'And still you refuse to ask me to take you?'

She bit into her lip, speech beyond her.

'It is a shame, Annie, because I would love my cock to be here, instead,' he pushed his finger in harder, faster and she cried out at the sharp sense of invasion—the welcome feeling of having any part of him inside her. She wanted to tell him she wanted that too, but whenever she opened her mouth to say it, she held back. They were playing a dangerous game, and if Annie were to concede so early, to give away her power, she knew she'd live to regret it. He was trying to break her. He was trying to get her to admit that no matter what he said or did, she would fall in with his plans, that she would be his again, and she instinctively knew she had to fight that.

'Since when do you need a handwritten invitation?' she muttered. 'Are you telling me you make every woman you sleep with beg for you?'

'Oh, no, Annie, this is just about you,' he said, confirming her thoughts. 'I want *you* to beg for me. I want you to admit that you still want me. I want the woman who acted like I meant *nothing* to prove herself wrong…'

'I've told you,' she moaned, as he moved his finger faster, and tilted her head back, eyes clinging to the ceiling as a wave of pleasure spread through her body. 'I—can't—'

'You can't what?'

Pleasure built, intense, fast, hard. 'Beg me, Annie,' he said, pulling his finger out, so she whipped her head forward, staring at him, heart racing. 'All you have to do is ask me to take you, and I will make you feel better than you've ever known possible.'

The throb in her gut demanded that of her. She needed him; what was the harm in admitting it? *Please.* Such a simple word and yet when she opened her mouth, it wouldn't come out. He stared at her, his own cheeks slashed with colour, so she knew he wasn't unaffected by this, that it was taking a degree of willpower all of his own.

'Please,' she said, and then, added quickly, 'stop. Stop now.'

His eyes widened with surprise and his lips clamped together to form a grim line, but he did what she'd said, every part of him growing still, and then Annie's heart sank as he pulled his hands away from her, his chest moving though with the force of his breathing.

'Is this really what you want?' she asked sadly, her heart heavy. 'Do you need to demean me, by hearing me beg, because five years ago I had the nerve to break up with you?'

'I don't give a shit that you dumped me, Annie. That's always been your prerogative.'

She tilted her chin, ignoring the way pain seemed to slice through her.

'It's your reason for ending it that I think pathetic. To leave someone, when you are grown woman, because your mummy and daddy don't think he's good enough? It's my own fault, but I did think better of you.'

She flinched.

'I was wrong. You're just as superficial as them. What is that expression about apples and trees?'

She glanced sideways, trying to catch her breath. It was a body blow, even though he'd used a few short words.

'You don't know what you're talking about.'

'I know that you were a coward then, by not standing up to your parents, and you're a coward now, for not admitting how much you want me. You live your life with your head in the sand—I'm disappointed in you, Annie.'

She ground her teeth, trying not to react, but she could feel her emotions spiralling out of control. Given the choice between anger, and showing how hurt she was, she firmly chose the former. 'Seriously, Theo, just go to hell.'

He leaned closer then, his eyes locked to hers, somber and intense. 'Are we not both already there, Annie Leonidas?'

CHAPTER SEVEN

A WEEK AFTER arriving on the island and Annie was in the worst mood of her life—and it didn't take a genius to work out why.

Ever since that passionate encounter in the kitchen, on the morning of the broken coffee cup, Theo hadn't touched her. He'd been cold, reasonably polite when necessary, but also distant. Despite that, Annie couldn't stop. She couldn't stop *wanting* him. What had started in that kitchen had ended in dramatic fashion, and she'd tried so hard to hold on to her anger. It was still there, stirring around in her belly, but more and more there was just a static electricity sort of awareness of every single movement Theo made.

Sleeping in the same bed and diligently not touching was its own form of torture. She'd barely let herself drift off because she was so worried her subconscious would take over and drive her towards him in the middle of the night.

Theo, meanwhile, either knew how distracted she was, or had no clue and didn't care. Either way, he swam naked each morning, so it had become her guilty pleasure to get up as soon as she heard the front door click shut, creep into the kitchen and watch him walk, glorious and raw, towards the ocean, to disappear into it, all beautiful man-hood and masculinity.

If he knew she watched, he didn't say. He left her mostly to herself, and Annie therefore set about read-ing her way through the small collection of books she'd found on a shelf, and pretending not to notice him, even when she was focused on him with a laser-like intensity.

There were a million things she wanted to ask him. To learn about his life since they'd parted, to understand him better, but she had barely any opportunities to ask those questions—even if she'd thought he'd be receptive.

They didn't eat together—the fridge was well stocked, so she simply grabbed what she wanted when she was hungry and out of an abiding sense of pride, tried to pre-tend her husband didn't exist.

But a sense of needing him, aching for him, craving him, was driving her almost mad.

So finally, on the eighth day of their 'honeymoon', she snapped. Maybe it was that same sense of pride, or maybe it was just lust. She knew only that he thought he could call all the shots, and she was sick of it. He wanted her to beg for him? Well, maybe she wanted that, too. Maybe she wanted him to admit that he was as power-less in the face of their attraction as she was. Or maybe she just wanted to pull apart his defenses, to strip him to his most animalistic self, to see the real man, not this edifice he was presenting her with.

Watching from the kitchen window as he carelessly strode towards the ocean, all stunning naked masculin-ity, she ground her teeth together, as a plan born purely of instincts formed.

Moving before she could properly think it through,

and certainly before she could second-guess herself, Annie stripped out of the T-shirt she'd slept in and then, before she could hesitate, the shorts as well, but she stopped short of removing her underpants. She wanted to give him his just desserts, to subject him to the same temptation he'd been throwing at her all week, but she wasn't quite as daring as him.

Still, dressed in just a skimpy pair of briefs, with her dark hair pulled over one shoulder, she stepped out of the front door and on autopilot, looked left and right, before grimacing at her silliness—because there was no one else there. It was a totally private island. She picked her way over the stones that were inlaid between the lawn, and then, to the sandy grass that gave way completely to the shoreline. He was swimming away from her, powerful strokes taking him in the opposite direction.

Good.

Let him swim, she thought, refusing to listen to common sense and turn tail back into the house.

The truth was, she was almost being driven mad by the way he was ignoring her. Infuriated and yes, hurt. Her ego was smarting by the way he appeared to have simply turned off any awareness of her, while she'd been drowning in the distraction of wanting.

So today, she'd see.

He saw her head, at first, though initially he didn't realise it was a person, just something in the ocean, not too far in front of him. But he slowed and took a second look, switched his stroke so he could keep his head above water, and then, he saw her face, too, in profile, her lips parted, her eyes closed, as she breathed in deeply. And then, she stood up, which brought her body just a little above the water's surface. Just enough to suggest that she too was naked, the top of her breasts revealed to him, so he cursed and stopped swimming, his first instinct being to turn right around again.

But perhaps with his subtle change in movement, something drew her attention, because she turned her head, towards him, her intelligent, clear eyes landing on his face, her soft, pink lips parted as though she were silently begging him after all.

Awareness was like a lightning bolt right to his cock.

When they'd been dating, he'd been so determined to respect her boundaries. Theo had never had any issues falling right into bed with a woman before, but Annie had been different. She'd been different from the first, but then, on her eighteenth birthday, when she'd begged him to kiss her, he'd known she was vulnerable and sweet, and that he'd do anything to protect her. It was the first time he'd felt like that in a long time—the first time he'd *ever* felt like it for someone in his new life. These people were all rich and spoiled, but Annie…not Annie.

He'd wished her a happy birthday, then kept an eye on her for the rest of the night—from a distance. Making sure she didn't ask anyone less scrupulous, and get taken advantage of.

Her twenty-first birthday had been different.

On her eighteenth, he'd known it was a dare. A silly game to seduce the man who'd once been the boy from the wrong side of the tracks. But it hadn't mattered. At eighteen, she'd been too young and innocent anyway. By twenty-one, when she'd asked again, it hadn't been a dare. She'd wanted him, and he'd presumed her to have the experience to know that she was playing with fire—and to welcome the consequences. So he'd kissed her, and tasted her, and he'd been hooked from that moment on.

Yet he hadn't slept with her. Even when they'd gone beyond that night, and started dating—secretly, because she hadn't wanted her parents to know—he'd somehow just understood that he wanted to silo what they were off from his other short-term relationships.

She was different, and he'd treated her as such.

But now, she was his wife. His goddamned wife, and she was staring at him like that, across the ocean. A wave bobbed past her, above her breasts, and then the ocean sucked out a little, so the water fell, and he saw her nipples, dusky pink, like her lips, peaked in the middle of her small, rounded breasts.

Slowly, he swam towards her, trying to bring his body back under control, to fight the surging heat of desire pounding him from the inside out. But what was the point? Hadn't she come here to tempt him? To do exactly this to him?

When he was close to her, just a foot or so away, he stopped swimming and stood, his eyes probing hers, studying her, his hands aching to reach out and touch. He waited for her to say something, but she was breathing hard, as though she'd just run a marathon.

As though she was nervous.

Or something.

'Did you feel like a swim?' he prompted.

She bit into her lower lip.

'Or something else?'

Her eyes lifted to his, her expression uncertain.

For God's sake, why was she tormenting him like this?

All she had to do was ask him to make love to her, and he would, all day and all night, until this damned beast of need was finally slayed, satiated. It was the only way to end this.

'Damn it, Annie, why are you here, naked?'

'I'm not naked,' she said, her voice a husk, in the early morning. 'And I thought it was just what we did here.'

He arched a brow. 'Does it offend you?'

He gestured to his chest, inviting her to look. She did. Her gaze dropped lower, her tongue darting out and licking her lower lip, so his cock jerked and his gut tightened.

Slowly, she shook her head, and then lifted a trembling hand, slowly, pressing it to his chest. 'I guess I just got sick of looking.'

He sucked in a sharp breath. Her touch was so tentative, so innocent, and yet it was also the most erotic thing he'd ever known.

'How exactly are you not naked?' he asked, the words bitten out, gruff and deep.

Her hand dropped from his chest, to lace with his fingers, which she pulled towards her hip, so he felt the elastic of her thong and bit back another curse.

'That seems tokenistic, at best.'

Her lips flicked in a small smile—a genuine smile, so for a second, he was back in the past, and she was just Annie. His Annie.

Until she wasn't. Until she was taken away from him—until she walked away from him, rather than standing up to her rich, entitled parents. She was nothing like he'd thought, because the Annie he'd held up on a pedestal was not the kind of woman to end it with a guy just because her parents told her to.

The memory was a timely reminder of who she was—and why this had to happen on his terms. He wouldn't let himself feel anything for her again. He wouldn't let her get under his defenses.

'Why did you come out here?' he said again.

'I told you—'

'No, Annie.' He pulled his hand back, glad for the shift in his feelings, glad for the way the past had reared its head at just the right moment, to reinforce why he had to keep his cool. 'You cannot get out of it that easily. If you want to touch, touch. But if you want me to fuck you, you're going to have to ask.'

She gasped, the hurt on her features something he wished he didn't see, and didn't care about, but the past was a complex beast, and tangled up in his anger and disappointment with her was the warmth he'd once held, too. The understanding of her—more of an understanding than he'd probably ever allowed himself to feel for another person.

'Why are you like this?' she asked, her features still pinched.

'Why do you think?'

'Your upbringing? Did someone hurt you? I don't know, Theo. You were always a closed book about your past—'

'My past? Annie, don't be obtuse. If you're wondering why I'm like this, then look in a goddamned mirror.'

Another gasp, this time, with her hand lifting to cover her lips. 'Don't say that.'

'I thought we agreed to be honest.'

She flinched.

'You were the first person in my life I ever really cared

about,' he said, almost conversationally, aware that the words had washed through him so often they'd lost their power to cut him now.

'What about the Georgiadeses?'

'I liked and respected them, and that was mutual. I did not care for them like I did you. And you discarded me without a backwards glance, because your parents asked you to.'

She shook her head. 'I didn't, it wasn't—'

'You did, and it was,' he contradicted fiercely. 'But don't worry—I'm glad. You showed me who you really are. What you really value. And you also reminded me of something I already knew but somehow, had let myself forget.'

She stared up at him, blinking quickly.

'I don't like people,' he said, and then, he reached out and put his hands on her hips, pulling her to him, so his cock nestled against the fabric of her pants, but his chest was hard to her soft, rounded breasts. 'I particularly don't like rich people.' His lip lifted in a cynical smile, as he saw the way her eyes shifted, the inner battle she was waging between her mind's indignation and her body's needs.

'You're rich,' she pointed out, voice trembly.

'No, I have money. It's not the same thing. You were born rich, and you have the prejudices to prove it.'

'I hate you,' she whispered, and in that moment, he knew she really did mean it.

'Yes, but you still want me.'

She looked away from him, her breath held, her chin angled in a pose of pure defiance, before she glared up at him, her eyes practically fulminating with rage. 'Yes,' she said, finally. 'I do.'

It was hardly the plea he'd been hoping for and yet, it was enough. It was more than enough. It was still a concession for her, that no matter what she might think of him, desire was ravaging her as it was him. He could only wish he wasn't stuck in the same metaphorical boat.

'But you want me, too,' she said, with a hint of angry resentment.

He stared down at her, admiration shifting in his chest. 'Do you need to hear me say it, Annie?'

She bit into her lip, a lip he was desperate to taste for himself, and nodded once, but her eyes were awash with uncertainty.

'I have no problem admitting that I want you.' He leaned closer, his voice brushing her ear. 'I am not a coward.'

'Do you really think that?' she asked, lifting one of her small hands and pressing it to his shoulder, like she was trying to physically shake him.

'I did, Annie. But coming to me for help was brave. Marrying me was braver still.'

Her eyes flicked to his, and she opened her mouth to say something, but he forestalled it.

'Then again, we both know there's no limit to what you'd do to keep your daddy happy.'

Her eyes shut as his words hit their mark—and he wished, almost more than he'd ever wished for anything, that he could take them back.

'Just shut up and fuck me,' she whispered then, blinking her gaze open and letting it land on his. And then, the word he thought he'd wanted and quickly came to despise, fell from her mouth: 'Please.'

He blotted out the horrible feeling spreading through him, ignoring anything but this. Later, he'd work out why he felt like a part of him was being torn to shreds. For now, he just wanted to experience this woman—this pleasure he'd denied himself, the whole time they'd dated.

'Good, Annie,' he murmured, lifting her higher in the water, and he kissed her as he wrapped her legs around his waist, supporting her weight, his hard body seeking her, needing her, so he broke the kiss only long enough to say, 'Are you on the pill?'

She nodded quickly, her cheeks flushed, her lips parted. 'Yes.'

'Thank Christ,' he groaned, nudging aside her briefs and then saying, for good measure, 'I'm clean. I presume—'

'Of course,' she said, and then, she hesitated, so he waited, though it was an agony not to plunge into her. He still waited, for her to say whatever she was thinking. She stared down at him and then, on a sob, repeated those awful words, 'Please, Theo, please.'

He drove into her with all the desperate, angry, years-old need that had been tormenting him right to his core. It was not gentle, and it was not soft, it was the act of a man driven by passion, who felt that answering need from his would-be lover.

But the second he thrust into her and she cried out, not in pleasure, but from pain and discomfort, and her face contorted, he connected her tightness with the cause of it and swore, staring at her face, his body buried too deep in her to move, to take it back. Anger though was firing through him, along with a sense of confusion.

'What the hell?'

She glared at him.

'You were—are you a virgin?'

'Well, not now,' she snapped with an impressively withering tone, given the situation, and digging her heels into his back and shifting a little, moving on his length so he had to reach for her hips to hold her still, because the pleasure was too good, and he needed to damn well think.

'You're telling me you were a virgin until a minute ago?'

'So what?'

'So what?' He stared at her, disbelief a whip, slashing through him. 'How the hell—'

'Can we possibly talk about this later?' she asked, her cheeks flushed, lips parted, as she moved again, and this time, he let her. Hell, he couldn't take it back, even if he wanted to.

'Damn it, Annie, we are going to talk about it,' he muttered, but he began to move, this time, more gently, slowly, careful to give her time to adjust to the fullness, to the feeling of being with a man for the first time.

He was still reeling from that, when she dug her nails into his shoulder and snapped, 'No, Theo, not like this. Don't treat me like you might break me. I want you to take me. I want you to treat me like you would if I was any of the woman you usually sleep with.'

He ground his teeth together, knowing instinctively he could never do that, because even now, Annie was different.

Not just because she was his wife, but because she was Annie; it would always be more complicated between them.

'Please,' she whispered, and he grimaced at the sound of surrender in her voice, at the knowledge that he'd taken something that should have been born of mutual passion—begging one person to pleasure them, and be pleasured in return—and turned it into a power play that she resented.

He felt the world spinning, out of his control, the decisions and instincts he always listened to now suddenly seeming questionable.

'Theo,' she said, sharply, so he gave up on thinking, questioning, analysing and wondering and just lost himself in her, and this, until she tipped over the edge and he held her shaking, trembling body against his own, murmuring reassurances in Greek, until her breathing returned to normal and he could trust himself to speak again.

Then, he pulled out of her, still rock hard and aching for his own release, and eased her down, so she could stand on the ocean's floor. The water was much deeper for her than him, so he kept his hands on her hips, in case a wave came that she needed to be lifted over.

But Annie could hardly meet his eyes. He ignored the pang of something rolling through him, hardening himself to anything like pity or doubt.

Nonetheless, he heard himself ask, albeit grimly, 'Are you hurt?'

She shook her head. 'I told you, I don't want you to treat me like—'

'It was your first time,' he said, swallowing back another curse as the reality of that landed like a thud against his chest. He didn't want to wonder why. He didn't want to question any of the suppositions he'd made about her lifestyle and choices in the years since they'd dated. Instead, he focused on his anger with her, at having been caught out like this. 'It should not have happened here, like this. It should not have happened with me.'

She closed her eyes, so her lashes were two dark crescents against her cheek. 'Why not?'

'Because it is a beach… It is—'

'Why not with you?'

He dragged a hand over his jaw. 'Because you hate me, for one,' he reminded her crisply.

'Yes, but you're also my husband.'

'Do you think I would have married you if I'd known?'

'Yes,' she said, grimacing. 'But I don't think you would have slept with me.'

A blinding light of clarity exploded before his eyes. 'You did this on purpose.'

Her eyes lifted to his and clung there a moment.

'You chose not to tell me.'

'Would you have slept with me, if you'd known?'

'Of course not. I have no interest in virgins.'

She frowned. 'Is that why you wouldn't sleep with me, back then?'

He thought back to that time, to how much he'd wanted her, yet had resisted, and he couldn't say why, except it had felt somehow important to wait. To show her that she was different to the many women he'd slept with before her.

But he was quiet too long, and apparently Annie drew her own conclusions from his silence. 'Well, I'm sorry to disappoint you, but if you thought I'd gone and gathered a heap of experience in the last five years, you were wrong.'

'You are twenty-seven,' he said, shaking his head.

'I'm aware of that.'

'I'm just trying to understand—'

'Well, maybe you shouldn't,' she said, but her voice wobbled a bit, belying the anger she was trying to infuse into her words. 'Maybe you should just stick to what you're good at and keep being an arrogant bastard.' She sniffed, and he had a sinking feeling that she was about to cry.

Hardly how he would have wanted her first time—or any woman's—to go. Guilt tore through his gut, along with a very familiar sensation from his childhood. A sense of not being able to keep precious things and people safe, of not being able to do the right thing by anyone. Of being not good enough.

'Excuse me, but I've had enough swimming for one day.' He didn't look back over his shoulder to see if she was following him; he told himself he didn't care, either way.

CHAPTER EIGHT

'WE'RE LEAVING FOR Athens in an hour,' he said, later that morning, interrupting a long stretch of silence that had been seriously grating on Annie's last nerve. Yet she hadn't dared be the first one to break it. Not after the beach.

Sex with Theo had been paradigm shifting. Wonderful, physically. Fulfilling and perfect and achingly good. But it had also been complicated and awful, because of how it had been afterwards. The accusation in his voice, the anger. She'd felt like a total inconvenience, and it was all she could do to remember the moment he'd pulled out of her, clearly without experiencing his own climax, and started tearing strips off her.

Except, he hadn't been mad, he'd been confused and judgemental, and she'd felt like a child who'd been caught doing the wrong thing.

'Annie, did you hear me?'

She glanced up at him slowly, then nodded.

'The silent treatment?' he said, the same scathing tone in his voice that made her feel like a misbehaving teenager.

'Fine.' She pasted a saccharine smile on her face. 'Thank you for consulting me, by the way.'

He stared at her, obviously pissed. 'Well, Annie, would *you* like to stay on this island another night, after what just happened?'

'What just happened?' He dragged a hand through his hair. 'We had sex—isn't that what you wanted?'

'It's what we both wanted.'

'I'm not saying otherwise. But what about my virginity changes the fact we both knew what we were doing?'

'*I* didn't. You took away my ability to know and act accordingly.'

'It's just sex,' she spat out.

'Your first time is different.'

'I never had you pegged for such a romantic.'

'It's not romance, it's—' But he faltered, and she knew she'd caught him out. 'Just how it is.'

'Oh, really? Was your first time some big, special, candlelit affair?'

He made a noise of dark amusement. 'Hardly.'

'So, what's the problem? Why the double standards?'

'Because you deserved better,' he shouted, silencing her, so she blinked up at him, and he frowned, shaking his head, like he wanted to take the words back.

And was it little wonder? He was still so angry with her, angry enough to blackmail her into this marriage, and yet there he stood, admitting that she deserved better? 'That's why I didn't sleep with you back then, Annie. I wanted your first time to be special. I wanted you to understand that *you* were special. I wanted you to know that I saw it, and would wait for you, that nothing mattered more to me than taking care of you. And even though that was many years ago, and I feel very, very differently now, apparently, there is still a part of me that cares. That wants to know you have what I believed you deserved in life, even when I have no interest in being the one to provide it.'

The words took her breath away. They sucked the life from her. The very oxygen she needed to exist seemed to evaporate like dew on a leaf.

'It was special,' she whispered, because it had been. Somehow, making love to Theo in the elemental, passionate ocean, the ancient, time-worn water washing over them, was like a baptism of sorts. A cleaning of the slate—a new start. She stood up, a little uncertain, but also, driven by his honesty to be honest with him.

'I cared about you, too, Theo. I know you don't believe that, because of how—and why—everything with us ended. You asked why I'm a virgin?'

His jaw shifted as though he were grinding his teeth, but he nodded.

'It's because of you,' she said, pressing a hand to his chest. 'When I was eleven and you came to live next door, I thought you were the most beautiful person I'd ever seen. When I was thirteen, I thought I was in love with you. I have a whole notebook somewhere in my room with Annie Leonidas scrawled all over it.' Her smile was rueful, but Theo stood still, completely frozen to the spot. 'When I was sixteen, I couldn't get you out of my mind. By the time I turned eighteen, I was yours for a song. Do you know how long it took me to work up the courage to ask you to kiss me?'

'You were drunk.'

'Yes. I thought it would give me courage, and it did.' He stared down at her.

'After that, I dated other guys. My parents set me up

with the sons of some of their friends,' she said, aware of the way his body tightened.

'Suitable men,' he said grimly.

She nodded, because that was exactly how they'd described the men to her. Men who came from families like theirs. Old families, aristocratic and wealthy, with proud names and coats of arms. Annie had known for as long as she'd been alive that the expectation was to marry just such a man. 'But I couldn't get you out of my head. So, by twenty-one, you were the sum total of fantasies and crushes, the only man I'd ever wanted. And when you kissed me, I just knew.'

'What did you know?' His voice had a hard quality to it, despite the way she was opening her heart to him.

'That I wanted you to be my first.'

'You aren't saying you've been waiting for me.'

'No.' Her lips twisted in a grimace. 'After things with us ended, and…everything with my mum… I just wasn't interested in dating. I've become quite reclusive,' she admitted.

'You should have told me.'

She bit into her lip. 'I didn't know how.'

He nodded, slowly, but when he reached out and pressed a finger to her chin, his touch was so gentle that his words, when he spoke, seemed totally jarring. 'It doesn't change anything, Annie. Sex is just sex to me, and you will always be who you became the morning you left. I can't forgive it. I don't want to.' He padded his thumb over her lower lip, evidently with no idea how hard she was finding it to breathe, much less remain upright.

'You know why I left,' she said, unevenly.

He dropped his hand away. 'Yes.' The word was laced with anger. 'I understand your reasoning.'

'You're still so angry.'

A muscle jerked in his jaw. 'I'm angry at myself, not you.'

'Why?'

'Because I should have known better than to let it go so far. I have always been able to walk away—from anyone and anything. And then you…'

'What?' she asked, quickly.

'You made me forget, for a while, that's all.'

She wished she understood, but he'd always been so reluctant to speak freely, so cryptic in his answers. 'Don't you think we should talk about this?' she asked.

His eyes ran over her face, and for a second she thought he might relent, but then, he shook his head, just once, but it was a death knell to any hopes she might have had of his opening up to her in a meaningful way. 'There is no time. The plane will be here soon, and I have things to take care of before we leave. Pack your bag, Annie. Real life is calling.'

He was silent as the plane took off, and it did nothing to ease the stretching of her nerves. Annie felt like she was at sixes and sevens, with no idea which way was up. She knew only that she hadn't wanted to leave the island.

She had a feeling she couldn't shake that Theo was running away.

But why?

If it really was a case of 'sex being just sex', as he'd claimed, why should it be such a big deal? Did he realise the contradictions in what he said? One minute it was an easy, physical thing, the next, she deserved her first time to be 'special'. And what did that even mean? Did he think that having careful, slow sex in a bed with some other man would have been *more* special than what they'd done?

Irritation built inside of her, stretching like a rubber band, and yet she'd presumed it would stretch and then snap, eventually. She'd presumed that at some point, he'd look at her and say something, or reach for her, or they'd share a moment and things would return to a more normal footing.

But the flight was almost completely silent, as was the drive to his mansion, on the other side of town. At some point during their honeymoon, all of Annie's belongings had been relocated from her father's to Theo's, and she tried not to think about how that must have pained her dad. And how Theo had probably enjoyed that knowledge. Had probably organised it for that reason.

His hatred of her father—and late mother—was like a constant niggle in the back of her mind; so too her betrayal for being able to ignore it, and fall into the way of craving him, despite that.

When they'd made love, she'd thought the ocean was like a wiping clean of their past, a rebirth of sorts, but she'd been wrong. There was far too much water under the bridge for that.

He said she'd made him what he was. That her rejection was the reason he was so cold now, so famously ruthless. And for Annie? Theo had hurt her, too. Why hadn't he understood that she'd had no choice? Why hadn't he seen that her parents were acting out of love?

His resentment had scored marks deep in her heart.

Maybe it just wasn't possible for either of them to move past that.

Maybe she was stupid to even hope.

But why would she hope? This was a temporary arrangement, the purpose of which was to rebuild her family's company. Why did she need to heal their past? Was it just a case of wanting to know that Theo was alive, and no longer angry with her? Or was there something more at the heart of it?

From the minute they got back to Athens, Theo launched himself into work, leaving the house before seven each morning and often not returning until close to midnight. She knew he worked long hours—he was renowned for it—but she'd become so used to him on their honeymoon. Even when they were pretending not to notice one another, he'd always *been* there, in that enormous, open-plan beach house. She'd been able to glance up and see him, to hear him, to breathe in and taste him in the air if he happened to walk close enough. Now she had to put up with just seeing little signs of him—like his toothbrush and his coffee cup.

It was pathetic. The whole thing.

She was no wallflower, waiting to be acknowledged by her husband, on his terms. She refused to be that woman.

A week and a half after returning to the city, she gave up on sitting around waiting for things to change, and began to formulate a plan. He was a workaholic, which made it easy to know where to find him, at least. She dressed with care in a black mini dress, styled her hair in big loose waves, applied a minimum of make-up that included her dark red lipstick, and added a pair of killer heels before stepping out of his mansion and hailing a cab—though she supposed she could have taken her own car, she didn't want the hassle of parking.

He owned the entire building in which his office was located, and when the cab pulled to a stop at the bottom of it, she took a second to glance up, right to the top, where she knew Theo would be, and took a beat. She could go home again. She didn't have to do this.

But then what? Eighteen months was a very long time of living with someone whose very presence had the ability to set your nerve endings alight, and who also seemed determined to pretend to ignore you.

The security for the building was tight. She had to give her name, so she knew he'd be expecting her, which wasn't exactly as she'd planned it, but so what?

She caught the elevator to the top floor, where an elegant woman in a pale-coloured suit was waiting with a polite smile.

'Mrs Leonidas,' she greeted deferentially. 'Mr Leonidas is expecting you.'

Half of Annie's lip twisted in an amused smile at that. He hadn't been, until about two minutes ago?

'Thank you,' she said, falling into step beside the other woman to a set of double doors that led to the Theo's office. The assistant knocked once, and Theo was there, drawing the door inwards.

'Thank you, Helen,' he murmured, barely glancing at her.

He only had eyes for Annie, and it was a very necessary shot in the arm.

She strode into his office, heels clicking against the large pale tiles. When she was in the middle, she put a hand on her hip and turned to face him. But the way he was looking at her was so smouldering that she completely lost her train of thought.

'Did you wear that out in public?'

She glanced down at her admittedly very short dress, and shrugged, her eyes daring him to complain. Daring him to pick this fight.

'Is there something wrong with it?'

A muscle throbbed at the base of his jaw, but he wisely stayed quiet. 'What can I do for you?'

'I'd like to discuss the terms of our marriage.'

He crossed his arms over his chest. 'The terms of our marriage have already been agreed to. I have the contract to prove it.'

'I'd like to vary them.'

'That's not generally how contracts work.'

'What's the matter, Theo? Are you scared of what I'm going to suggest?'

'What do you want?' he asked, but stayed where he was, so for a second, she thought maybe she was right: that he *was* scared.

'Well, definitely not this.'

He arched a single brow. 'You knew what you were getting into when you agreed to marry me.'

'No, I don't think I did.'

'What precisely is the problem?'

'You're ignoring me.'

He frowned. 'Am I?'

She rolled her eyes. 'Don't gaslight me. We both know you're staying out of the house so you don't have to see me. What happened to a "public marriage"?'

He moved to his desk then, pressing his fingers into

the edge of it, his expression thoughtful. 'You'd like to go on more dates?'

'I'd like to not feel like I'm either walking on eggshells or being completely ignored.'

'You are the one who asked me to turn your father's company around.'

'I know that.'

'Did you think I would just snap my fingers? It takes work, *agape*. Long, hard work.'

Chastened, she bit into her lip. She'd barely thought about the company since he'd agreed to take it over and help her.

'I know.'

'Is this about dinner dates, Annie, or something else?'

Her heart began to race so loudly, it was all she could hear.

'It's about spending time together.'

He walked towards her then, his gait predatory, like a cougar, prowling, intent on his catch. 'I told you, sex wouldn't change anything.'

'And I told you, I get that.' She angled her chin belligerently. 'Why can't you take me at my word and accept that I can walk and chew gum at the same time.'

'What does that mean?'

'I can sleep with you, talk to you, and be fake married to you, without any part of this changing. In eighteen months, I will be demanding that divorce we've discussed, no matter what happens between us now. All I'm saying is: Why can't we just make the most of this, in the meantime?'

He stared down at her, as though she'd started speaking a totally foreign language.

'I'd never had sex before that day,' she said seriously, honestly, staring up at him. 'And now, you hardly seem to want to touch me. Did I do something wrong?'

Theo didn't move, so Annie's heart sank.

'I mean, I wasn't sure…'

'No.' His voice was rough. 'You did nothing wrong. It was fine.'

'Fine?' she squeaked, mortified.

'Great, okay? It was great.'

'Because you didn't—'

'No, I didn't,' he said. 'But that was not because you erred in any way.'

'It's just—I liked it. And I want—I would like—'

'More,' he said, moving a hand to her hip and placing it there, fingers splayed.

She nodded mesmerized. 'Yes.' It was a whisper. And an admission. It was also terrifying, because she felt so exposed to him, so raw and vulnerable. 'Yes, I want more. I want you.'

'Oh, Annie,' he groaned, dropping his head forward, like he was trying to blank her out. 'This has the potential to be very complicated.'

'Why? What's changed since that day in Sydney? You were fine with sex, then. What's different now?'

'You know what's changed. I presumed you were—if not exactly like me, at least experienced.'

'Get over it. My inexperience doesn't mean anything to me, it shouldn't to you. It's just…happenstance.'

He made a grunt, which could have been agreement or disagreement.

'If you don't want to sleep with me, okay, but I don't want to be married to someone who won't even talk to me.'

A muscle ticked at the base of his jaw as his eyes held hers for a long time. 'You know why we got married. So far as I remember, talking to one another was not a factor.'

She stared at him, hating how much his words hurt, hating that she couldn't properly conceal it. The fact he wasn't going to compromise was blatantly obvious, so she'd have to work out a way to get what she wanted. Which was to know her husband. To have him get to know her again, too. 'Fine. Then I want to stick to the original deal—a public marriage, like you suggested. I want to go for lunch with you.'

His expression was practically a scowl. 'Lunch?'

'You've heard of the concept, I presume?'

'Today?'

'It is lunchtime, isn't it?'

'Wearing that?'

'What's wrong with this dress? I've seen photos of the women you usually date—I know what you like.'

He looked her up and down, shaking his head once. 'That's not— Annie—'

'If you don't want to eat with me, just say. I'll go somewhere on my own.'

She could see his cogs turning, and knew enough now about Theo to recognise that jealousy was shifting through him. 'No,' he said, sharp and decisive. 'I'll take you to lunch. It's fine.'

It sounded anything but fine, yet Annie didn't focus on that—she chose to take this for the victory it was. Theo was going to stop ignoring her, right now. Because Annie had a feeling there was so much more about him she didn't understand, so much she didn't know. Back then, she hadn't had a single clue how to scratch beneath the surface. He'd so easily been able to shut down her lines of enquiry, by just changing the subject or diverting her attention. Annie was older and wiser now, and she wasn't going to let him get away with it this time.

Operation Get To Know Her Husband was about to get underway.

CHAPTER NINE

THE ROOFTOP BAR of the fashionable boutique hotel boasted an exclusive clientele and stunning views of the Acropolis. The menu was unapologetically Greek, and their table private, set on the corner of the terrace, with a concrete planter filled with spiky green plants separating them a little from the other diners. In the background, there was a low hum of conversation and the soft strains of jazz music, the husky acoustic singing ringing with emotion.

She could imagine this place would be packed at night, filled with Athens's elite, here to see and be seen. On one level, it surprised her that Theo had brought her to a place like this. Then again, a lot had changed in five years. She didn't really know that much about the man she'd married, which was the whole point of this lunch.

'Your usual, sir?'

Annie blinked across at Theo, surprised by the waiter's question. Evidently, Theo came here often enough to have a 'usual'. With a date?

Of course with a date. She knew he'd hardly been a monk since they parted ways.

'Would you like a cocktail?' Theo asked Annie.

She glanced at the waiter, and nodded. 'An Aperol, thanks.'

The waiter nodded once then left.

'You come here often?'

'It is close to the office.'

She frowned. 'So you come for…work lunches?'

His smile was tight. 'Something like that.'

Annie suppressed a sigh. That hardly told her anything. Five years ago, Theo had been reluctant to share anything too personal, but he had at least made conversation. Now it was like getting blood from a stone. But she'd expected that. She just had to warm him up a little.

'How are things going with the company?'

His frown was reflexive. 'It's a mess.'

Her brows shot up. 'That bad, huh?'

'I'm still trying to work out if it's a case of incompetence or—'

'Or?' she asked when he broke off mid-sentence.

The waiter returned with a tray and two drinks, placing them down. Both Theo and Annie waited until they were alone again.

'Or something more serious.'

'You're talking embezzlement?'

'Possibly. Fraud. I'm not sure. I have a team of forensic accountants going through your books now.'

Annie squeezed her eyes shut on a wave of nausea. 'Oh, God.'

'You didn't suspect?'

'I didn't know how everything got so bad, so quickly, but my involvement is peripheral at best—I hired someone who came very highly recommended to run the company. By the time I realised we were over-leveraged, it was too late.'

'What about your father?' he asked with obvious contempt.

Annie bit into her lip, hating how much Theo despised the older man, even when she understood his reasoning. 'He hasn't been the same, since Mum…'

Theo's eyes rested on Annie's face a long time, before he glanced towards the view. 'That was a long time ago.'

'There's no statute of limitations on grief, apparently.'

Theo turned back to Annie. 'And you, Annie?'

'What about me?'

'I imagine you were also grieving.'

A constriction formed in her throat, making it hard to swallow. She nodded quickly, then took a sip of her drink. It was sweet and sparkly. 'She'd been sick for six months, though. I hoped she'd get better, but at the same time, I was prepared that she wouldn't. She wasn't the same after the first heart attack.'

Theo's eyes narrowed. He knew the timing of it. Annie had told him, the morning she'd ended things. She'd explained that her mother was so devastated by the idea of their being together she'd had an actual heart attack.

'You understand that it was not your fault?' Theo asked, echoing something he'd said at the time. Only back then, he'd grabbed her arms and pulled her to his chest, his face lined with passion, with a need to make her understand. Now he was the opposite, cool and calm, asking almost like he didn't care one way or the other.

'We'd argued,' she whispered, pressing her fingertips to her temple, reliving that awful night. 'They'd insisted we break up, I was blindsided. I mean, I knew you weren't who they expected me to be with, but they'd never been so overt in telling me what to do.' She shook her head, oblivious to the way his eyes narrowed, and his lips formed a compressed line of disapproval. 'I was surprised and I probably overreacted.'

He made a sound of disapproval. 'You were twenty-two years old.'

'But you know, the situation with Mary,' she whispered. 'Ever since she died, they spent every ounce of energy protecting me, carving out the life they thought I should lead, to keep safe.'

'What point is life if you do not actually live it?'

She'd lived it with Theo. For that one perfect year, Annie had felt as though she were brimming with vitality. As though she had a purpose beyond standing in for Mary, was seen as someone other than a poor replacement.

'They had my best interests at heart.'

'How can you say that, even now?'

'It's true. I know it must seem over-the-top to you, Theo—'

'To anyone with eyes or a brain.'

'Thank you for that.'

He leaned forward, surprising her by putting a hand on hers. 'You were right to stand up to them. If only you'd had the courage to see it through.'

She bit on her lip, looking across at him, her heart racing wildly. She ignored the condemnation in the way he'd accused her of lacking courage—like he had any idea how strong she'd had to be, all her life—and focused instead on his implication. 'And what would have happened, if I had?' she asked, toying with her napkin.

She sensed his withdrawal, even before he removed

his hand and returned it to his glass. 'I don't deal in hypotheticals.'

'Indulge me,' she rebuffed.

'For what reason? We'll never know what our future might have been had they not interfered. Had you felt that our relationship was important enough to fight for.'

She looked across at the Acropolis, but for once took no solace in the ancient, familiar stones.

'You have no idea what my life was like,' she said, unevenly, toying with her napkin.

'I knew you.'

'No, I'm starting to think that's not true.' Her brain was shifting from one spark to another, connecting dots, so when she looked at Theo now, it was with a dawning comprehension. 'You hid yourself from me, you know. Anytime I asked about your childhood, your life before you came to live next door, you would change the subject.'

His nostrils flared.

'But maybe I did the same thing,' she pondered, lips pulled to the side. 'I mean, I told you Mary died, but I didn't tell you what that did to me. What it did to my parents, and how they treated me. I didn't explain to you that I spent my entire life knowing that they wished our places had been reversed. Or that my intrinsic value wasn't in me, personally, but in being their last surviving daughter. My mother would say to me, every night, that she couldn't handle it if anything ever happened to me. That I had to stay safe and stay alive, just for her. Do you have any idea how terrified I was to even cross the street, Theo? The pressure of it, their expectations—that's been my *entire* life.'

He was watching her with an expression that gave nothing away, but Annie wasn't really seeing him, anyway. 'I love them, so much, but I also…it's hard to forgive them, for how they were with me. And how they were with you,' she admitted.

'And yet you still do his bidding.'

'With the company, you mean?'

'You were so desperate to save it, for your father's sake, that you agreed to marry a man you profess to hate.'

'The company is all he has left.'

'He has you.'

'I don't know if he really even sees me, anymore,' she whispered. 'Since Mum, it's just been…'

She searched for the right words and drew a blank. The truth was, it had been hollow. Empty. 'Anyway…' She trailed off into nothing, grateful for the reappearance of the waiter to take their food orders. Though she hadn't even looked at the menu and instead appealed to Theo to choose for her.

He ordered a selection of things, and by the time they were alone again, Annie had resolutely pushed the grief of her own life aside. She hadn't come here to unburden herself to Theo, but rather to find out more about him.

'That's my sad story,' she said, tilting her head to the side and considering him. 'Now it's your turn.'

'Is that how this works?'

'Yes, usually. You know, conversation ebbs and flows.'

His smile was tight. 'I'm familiar with the concept.'

'But not particularly skilled with the execution.'

His next smile was more of a grimace. 'We can't all have your charm.'

She flinched, because it didn't come across as a compliment at all. He expelled an angry breath, then surprised her by saying, 'I'm sorry. I didn't mean that as it sounded.'

'Like you resent my "charm"?'

'In fact, I admire it,' he said, slowly, as though the words were dragged from him against his better judgement.

'Coming from the man who can walk into any room, say one word and have everyone fall silent to hear you speak?'

He let out a gruff laugh. 'Is that how you view me?'

'It's how everyone views you.'

'That's because I have money.'

'No, it's not that.'

'Believe me, it's a factor.'

'I grew up with money,' she demurred. 'Surrounded by it, in fact. Your charisma is regardless of your bank balance.'

'Are you saying if I'd still been living on the streets, you'd have looked at me twice?' he pushed, his voice dark with resentment, so she felt a hum in her brain telling her she was close to a source of pain for him. And it wasn't that she wanted to cause him distress, but rather, to get to the heart of his life's experience, so she could better understand him.

'I don't deal in hypotheticals,' she volleyed back, with a small smile. He rewarded her with a flicker of his own lips, and her heart stammered. But she wouldn't be misdirected by a simple smile. 'How long were you on the streets for, Theo?'

She sensed it again; that immediate withdrawing, like

he was physically erecting a structure between them. 'Long enough.'

'A year? Two years? Four?'

'Does it matter?'

'Yes. I think it matters a great deal to you, and it matters to me, too.'

'Why?'

'Because it's a part of who you are.'

'I left that boy behind a long time ago.'

'Did you?' she pushed, pressing her elbows to the table and lacing her fingers together beneath her chin. 'Are you sure?'

His eyes bore into hers. 'What are you suggesting?'

'In the same way my life to this point has shaped me, so too has yours. It's incredibly naive to suggest that you can just shirk the bits of yourself you no longer want.'

'It's amazing what willpower can achieve.'

'Don't be glib.'

His nostrils flared. 'Did we come to lunch to examine my biography in detail?'

'Partly, yes,' she said honestly.

'Damn it, Annie, this isn't our deal.'

'It's not expressly prohibited by our contract,' she pointed out, then tried a different tack. 'What are you afraid of?'

'Nothing,' he denied.

'Then why not answer my questions?'

She'd laid a trap and he'd stepped right into it. She could see him weighing that up, considering it and she just hoped and prayed the waiter wouldn't come and interrupt, giving Theo an easy excuse to change the subject to something banal like the quality of the olive oil.

'I was in foster care from when I was three until I was seven, when I ran away for the first time. After that, I was mostly on the streets, except for a few occasions when I was arrested and returned to care. It never lasted long. By then, my manners were not particularly conducive to being looked after,' he said.

'What does that mean?'

'That I was very difficult. Aggressive, defensive, untrusting, angry. On the street, those qualities served me well, but in someone's home, it didn't tend to go over too well.'

'Oh, Theo,' she said, her heart breaking for the little boy he'd once been. 'Why did you run away, when you were only seven years old?'

For the briefest moment, she could have sworn he looked afraid. Desperate to end the conversation. And she was tempted to take pity on him and let it go. But this was all so crucial to understanding him, to understanding the decisions he made, even now, that she held her ground.

'Why do you think?'

'I couldn't say.'

'It's better to leave it.'

'Why?'

'There's no advantage to reliving that time.'

'Were you hurt, Theo?'

His eyes stayed locked to hers. 'It was not the first time I was hit, but it was by far the worst.'

She gasped, tears filling her eyes.

'See, Annie? Sometimes the truth is not really what you want.'

That was accurate. She didn't want this truth for him,

but the fact it had happened made her ache to comfort him. She pushed up out of her chair, going around to him, uncaring that they were in a restaurant. She needed to be close to him, and perhaps he felt that too, because she wouldn't have been able to sit in his lap without Theo pushing back from the table a little.

Her heart was splintering apart for that boy. Seven years old. 'I'm so sorry,' she whispered, catching his face in both hands, staring into his eyes. 'You should never have known that pain.'

'No,' he agreed. 'Nobody should.'

She dropped her head forward and pressed her lips to his forehead.

'I can't imagine what it was like,' she said, after a beat. 'Living on the streets…'

'For a start, that's a very sanitary euphemism for what it was like. Every day was a baptism by fire.'

She pulled away so she could look into his eyes. 'In what way?'

It was abundantly clear that Theo didn't want to have this conversation, but to his credit, he didn't hold back. 'The first month was the hardest. I was large for my age, but still just a boy. Skin and bone, and scared of the dark,' he admitted, lips twisting in a self-deprecating grimace. 'I begged, but one night, was mugged for what little I had, including my only pair of shoes,' he said. Annie's heart cracked apart. 'But a few weeks later, I met a man—little more than a teenager, actually—called Simon. He took me under his wing, along with a few other kids. He showed us where the good corners were to beg, how to steal from shops without getting caught.' Theo's Adam's apple bobbed as he swallowed. 'I hated stealing. Even then, I knew it was wrong, but I was so hungry. And Simon—while he cared for us, he also had the potential to lose his temper—spectacularly—if we didn't bring enough food or money back to him. After a few years, he and I fell out. We fought. I had to leave.'

'Leave?'

'I went to the other side of town. It was darker. Poorer. Rougher, but by then, I was at least able to take care of myself. I heard that Simon died a few months after I left,' he added, clearing his throat, so Annie knew, without him having to say it, that he somehow blamed himself. 'He got in a fight with someone bigger. He always had more bark than was wise, for someone his size. But I used to be there, to help. To defend him,' Theo admitted.

'But you were so much younger.'

'I was a quick learner. You have to be on the streets. I knew how to fight, to the death, if necessary.'

She gasped. 'Was it ever necessary?'

'Are you asking me if I have ever killed another person, Annie?'

She blinked, the thought one that had never occurred to her. She nodded slowly, but held her breath, and only let it out when he shook his head to indicate no.

'But back then, I would have, if I'd needed to. Maybe if I'd been with Simon, that afternoon, I would have, to save his life. I don't know. It was a different time, and I was a different person. Hunger, poverty, desperation— they change you.'

'I don't know,' she said, lifting a hand and curving it around his cheek. 'I don't think you're capable of it.'

'Don't you?'

She shook her head. 'Of defending someone, absolutely. But you're not violent, Theo.'

Their eyes held for a long time, and the longer they looked at one another, the more Annie felt a sense of conviction deep in her gut. She knew the real Theo. She always had done. She saw beneath whatever he projected and saw what was in his heart.

At least, she thought she had.

'I have never spoken about Simon,' he said, slowly, as if only coming to that realization himself.

Warmth spread through her. 'I'm glad you told me.'

'I have felt a sense of responsibility for a long time. I walked away from him, and I shouldn't have. I should have stayed. I knew what his temper was like. But by then, I had my own feelings and thoughts...'

'You couldn't have been with him twenty-four-seven.'

'No,' Theo agreed, but quietly, as though he wasn't convinced.

'You cared for him,' Annie prompted, remembering Theo's assertion, the day they'd left the island, that she, Annie, was the only person who'd ever inspired that emotion in him. Maybe that hadn't been entirely accurate.

'We were part of a team,' he said, with a small shake of his head. 'It's different. For all I felt it my obligation to defend him, to protect him, I expected nothing in return. I did not rely on Simon, I did not need him to need me. But I would have given my life to spare his, if I could have.'

Annie shuddered at the very thought of Theo having died as a teenager. 'What happened next?' she asked. 'Did you find another...team?'

'No, Annie. After that, I was resolutely alone. Until I met the Georgiadeses, and then, until I met you.'

Silence fell, heavy with the weight of their past, their difficulties, the hurt that each brought to this. And yet there was also a strange sense of peace flooding Annie, because for the first time, they were really connecting honestly and openly, about something of substance. He wasn't trying to shield her from the brutal reality of his childhood, and in hearing this truth, she felt like she would crack other parts of him open, too.

Annie stayed there, on his lap, as close to him as they could be in a public space, even when the waiter brought their food. She wasn't ready to relinquish this, and she was relieved—and delighted—that he evidently felt the same way.

But the longer she sat on his lap, the more her feelings morphed, from sympathy and concern to something far more grown up, her awareness of him, as a man, flooding her body. She dropped one of her hands to his chest, and pressed it there, feeling his warmth and strength, the hard beating of his heart.

'Why don't you not work late tonight?' she murmured, her eyes dropping to his lips. 'In fact, why don't you take the afternoon off?'

One side of his mouth lifted in a mocking half smile. 'Would you like to go shopping? Or perhaps to see a movie?'

She pulled a face. 'Neither of those things holds much appeal.'

'Then what were you thinking, Mrs Leonidas?'

Her heart turned over in her chest to hear him call her

that. 'I was thinking we could go home,' she said, letting her hand drift a little lower.

'Are there some more books you wish to read?'

She laughed. 'You're enjoying this.'

'Having my wife demand I take time off work to make love to her? Yes. I think I actually am.'

'Is that a "yes"?'

He looked at her long and hard, and she held her breath, wondering if he might be going to turn her down, despite the way the air was sparking with a mutual and consuming awareness.

'I have to work,' he said, gently easing her from his lap. At least she could hide the disappointment that was all over her face. 'But I will see you tonight, Annie.'

He had been so terrifyingly tempted to turn his ordered life on its head and go home with his wife. Not after lunch, either, but then and there. To toss a few hundred euros down on the table, throw her over one shoulder and storm his way to the waiting car. Hell, he wasn't even sure if they'd have made it home. Once in the confines of the back seat, he'd have probably wanted to sink right into her.

If he was honest with himself, he'd thought of little else since that morning on the beach, which was why he'd spent almost every waking minute hiding out in his office, avoiding her. Because if he couldn't see her, he couldn't reach for her, and beg her to come to bed with him.

It was just the same as always. Annie had a power over Theo that he refused to allow to take hold. Not again. Not even when she'd revealed such heartbreaking details about her life, explaining something he'd never quite understood: why her parents had such a hold over her. Why she'd simply agreed to break up with him, and let that be the end of it.

Then, talking about his past had only served to stir up the feelings that were the root cause of his approach to life. Every day had been loaded with danger and risk, uncertainty and insecurity. He hadn't known if he would find food, be in a fight, end up in jail—it had been a constant gamble. He'd needed to use all his wits to stay alive, and as much as he'd worked as part of a team led by Simon, he'd still retained his independence and autonomy, refusing to grow close to the other children, refusing to be comforted by their presence.

It really was only Annie who'd ever made him weak there, who'd drawn him in, made him think—for a brief year—that maybe life could be different after all.

And yes, he wanted her physically—and he would have her again, he accepted—but it wouldn't be because she asked and he came running. It would be on his terms. It had to be—it was the only way he'd make it out of this marriage unscathed. He had to call the shots, to know that he was part of their strange, transactional 'team', but that he was just as autonomous and independent as he ever had been. And most importantly, he could never forget who she was, who her father was, and how they viewed him. Nothing there would ever change.

CHAPTER TEN

ANNIE HAD NO idea what to expect. Theo had politely turned down her invitation, and she'd been smarting ever since, though she'd done her best to hide that for the rest of their lunch. The spirit of closeness was broken, though. They'd stuck to small talk, inconsequential and bland, and Annie had come home *alone*. Frustrated and alone.

So much for her little black dress working some kind of magic.

She'd done a workout in Theo's gym, gone for a swim, contemplated cooking something special for dinner but decided that was pointless when she'd probably end up eating alone, again. At some time around five, her father's housekeeper had texted to remind her that Elliot's birthday party was the following weekend. Annie might have been offended by the insinuation that she could forget, except it had actually completely slipped her mind, in the hubbub of her marriage.

She'd texted back that she'd be there, but when the housekeeper had asked about Theo, she'd immediately written back in the negative.

Theo hated her father—no way would she bring him to a birthday party in his honour. There was no need to poke that particular bear.

She was just contemplating another swim, when she heard the front door open, and every single cell in her body began to reverberate with anticipation. She moved on autopilot towards the lobby, so she saw the moment Theo stepped through the door, his eyes immediately landing on her.

Annie's lips were parted with surprise, her eyes widened, because after his rejection that afternoon, she'd presumed he'd stick to his usual routine of working until almost midnight.

'Does the offer still stand?' he asked, cutting out any need for small talk, any pretense that they both didn't know why he'd come home.

Her mouth went dry but she nodded quickly, then swallowed. 'Take me to bed, Theo. Please.'

His lips curled in something like genuine amusement and her heart slammed into her ribs. 'Princess, you are going to be begging me at the top of your lungs in a few minutes.'

'We'll see,' she replied impishly, so Theo surprised her by laughing, and stalked the rest of the way between them, before scooping Annie up in his arms and carrying her towards their bedroom, shouldering in the door then placing her on her feet.

'I'm disappointed you're not still wearing that goddamn dress,' he muttered.

She bit into her lip. 'I have to say, disappointment is not the response I was aiming for.'

He grinned. 'Wrong choice of word. I should have said, I haven't been able to stop thinking about how hot you looked in that thing.'

Pleasure spun through her. 'I can put it on again.'

'No. Don't do that.' His eyes were hooded when they met hers. 'I'm much more interested in what was under the dress, anyway.'

'Ah.' She smiled knowingly. 'Well, I think you'll find the same thing is under this as that.'

'I'd better make sure,' he said.

'Probably a good idea.'

His hands caught the hem of her T-shirt, but as he lifted it, he paused, a frown shifting his lips. 'Annie, remember what I said, after last time?'

Sex is just sex. She nodded. She'd remember forever.

'Good.' He kissed her forehead, so her heart went all mushy even when she tried to shield it as quickly as she could. 'I don't want there to be any miscommunication.'

'There won't be,' she assured him. She'd gotten the message loud and clear, and it was one she agreed with.

He pushed the shirt the rest of the way, over her body, his hands tracing its progress, roaming her breasts, her back, curving over her arse, as he lifted her and held her body to his. She couldn't simply stand there and be undressed, though. She also wanted to touch and feel, to know the perfection of his nearness. She pushed at the buttons of his shirt then slid it off his body, before leaning forward and kissing his shoulder. His skin was warm and smooth; she ran her lips over him, flicking his nipples with her tongue, before letting her hands find his belt and unfastening it.

He made a guttural noise from deep in his throat and an ancient, feminine pride trilled in her veins as he stepped out of his trousers and boxers so he was completely naked. She glanced down, her cheeks flushing at this now familiar sight of him—those early morning swims on the island had indelibly imprinted his form into her mind's eye.

'I don't know what to do,' she admitted softly, yet without fear. She trusted Theo, she realised. At least in this way. She knew he wouldn't judge her inexperience, that he'd help awaken this side of her.

'You must have some idea of what you'd like,' he said, as his hands roamed her body, touching, flicking, teasing, before he pushed at her shorts, so they ran down her legs, and she too was naked. She shivered then, simply because it was so intimate, so laced with promise.

'Show me?' she invited, her eyes hooked to his, so she saw the way his irises darkened and his lips parted on a hiss of breath.

'Yes, Annie,' he agreed. 'I'll show you,' and then he kissed her, his lips meshing with hers, their tongues duelling, as he lifted her easily and wrapped her legs around his waist, just as he had in the ocean. She rolled her hips, silently inviting him to take her again—how she'd loved that feeling—but Theo wasn't to be commanded. This was his show; he was as in control here as in the boardroom.

He moved to the bed, placing her in the middle of it. 'Lie down.' He stared at her, dragging his eyes over her body with a possessive heat that made her feel as though she was burning up. 'Good girl,' he murmured, when she lay on her back, and his praise made her skin lift with goosebumps. 'Now, let's try something,' he said, bringing his weight over her, so his nakedness was tantalisingly close.

'What?' she asked, lifting her hips again so that he shook his head and tsked.

'I want you to be completely silent,' he said, his grin showing his skepticism. 'Not a sound.'

'I thought you wanted to hear me scream your name?'

'That will come later,' he said, and she shivered in anticipation. 'Are you ready?'

She nodded, already submitting to his request for silence.

His eyes held a challenge, but then, his lips were on her collarbone, before dragging lower, to her breasts, his tongue flicking and rolling her nipples so that she arched her back and bit into her lip so hard she almost drew blood. A curse filled her mind, but she held it back—just.

'Good,' he murmured his approval against her stomach, as he dragged his mouth lower, until he was beneath her belly button. She pushed up onto her elbows, her jaw dropping when his hands gripped her thighs and spread them wide, so her most intimate self was revealed to his hungry gaze. 'So beautiful,' he said, his eyes slipping to hers almost accusingly, before his head dipped down and his tongue was running over her. She let out a heavy breath—not a noise, exactly, yet it was a sound of utter churning pleasure, and her fingers gripped his hair, simply because without holding on, she thought she might tumble all the way over the edge of the earth.

'Not a sound,' he reminded her, glancing up at her, before his mouth began to move again, sucking, tasting, discovering which buttons he could push, before moving one of his hands there so he could press two fingers inside of her.

'So wet,' he murmured. 'Do you want me?' he asked, as she pulsed around him.

She nodded, without speaking.

'How much?'

She glared at him, as the world began to shake, and pleasure was a radiant force.

'Say it,' he invited. 'I want to hear you now.'

'God, please,' she groaned, tilting her head back with relief. 'Don't stop. I want—I need—I need everything.'

'Yes,' he agreed. 'And I'm going to give it to you.' And he did. First, with his fingers, which sent her over the edge, so that she was trembling all over, before he brought his body over hers, his head level with hers, and his knee nudged her legs wide again, so he could press his cock to her sex.

'Ready?' he asked, stroking her head gently so that her heart trembled for a different reason. She nodded, dragging her nails down his back and digging them into his buttocks.

As he drove into her, he kissed the flesh just beneath her earlobe, and the sensations were almost too much to bear. He moved as though he'd been given the key to understanding exactly what she needed. Every time he shifted, he brushed new nerve endings, so she was almost exploding with the power of her pleasure, coming apart at every seam she possessed.

'Theo, Theo,' she said, over and over, forgetting that she'd once been determined never to give him that, never to show him how much she wanted him. 'Please,' she cried into the bedroom, not even caring that she'd probably see a look of triumph in his face, that he'd revel in her weakness.

When he dragged his mouth to her breast and took a nipple into his mouth, sucking on it until she saw stars,

Annie was gripped by a fierce orgasm, her whole body writhing from the force of her pleasure.

'You are so beautiful,' he muttered and then pulled out of her, moving to stand at the edge of the bed, staring down at her, so for a second, she feared history was repeating itself, and he wasn't going to experience his own pleasure. And she wanted him to. She wanted to know that he'd been as driven wild as she had been.

But then, he crooked a finger, indicating for her to stand up. Heart in her throat, she did so, going toe to toe with him. His hands on her hips were strong, commanding, as he turned her over, to face the bed, then pushed at her shoulders, guiding her so she was bent at the hips, her elbows braced on the bed.

'Remember what I said,' he asked, and before she could answer, he'd pushed into her again, this time, harder, faster, more like that first time, in the ocean, and his hands came around her body, one massaging her breast until she was crying out with the sensations he could so easily stir, and the other moving to her clit, brushing it as he took her from behind and made the whole world stop making sense. How could anything be the same once she'd known pleasure like this? How could *she* ever be the same?

She tried to remember what he'd said—sex was sex—but the truth was, this was mind-altering, personality-changing sex, and she would never be the same afterwards.

'Theo,' she cried out, but this time, her voice was drowned out by his own gruff, rasping cry into the air. After that, there was only the sound of their rapid breathing.

* * *

'Can I ask you something?' Annie murmured, her breath warm against his chest. His hand, stroking her back, stilled, but then, he began to trail his fingers once more over her soft, smooth skin.

Her voice was soft, and yet, something inside of him braced for her question. He'd shared more with her over lunch than he'd intended. She had an ability to reach inside of him and draw out whatever she wanted to know. 'Yes,' he said, though, after a beat.

'How did you come to live with the Georgiadeses?'

His hand began to draw invisible circles in the small of her back, as he replayed that time in his life. It felt like a lifetime ago.

'I was fifteen,' he said.

She propped her chin on his chest, her eyes resting on his face. 'I remember.' A quick glance at her showed a knowing smile, one he felt tugging at his own lips.

'You were eleven.'

'And totally smitten.'

His laugh surprised him.

'Anyway, that doesn't answer my question.'

'No.' He nodded once. It wasn't something he, or the Georgiadeses, had ever really discussed, but that didn't mean it was a secret. There was no reason not to tell Annie. 'Paul saw me shoplifting—just an apple and a bag of crisps. I stuffed them under my shirt. He followed me out of the store. I was going to run. I thought he'd drag me to the cops or something. Instead, he just asked me if I had somewhere to sleep.'

'Were you scared?'

He shook his head. 'You remember Paul. He had kind eyes and a gentle, patient voice.'

'Yes,' she agreed softly.

'He was older, too—in his seventies by then. He couldn't have hurt me, even if he'd wanted to.'

'He could have called the police, like you said.'

'I would have outrun him easily.'

'But you didn't.'

'No,' he frowned. 'And he surprised me, by asking if I wanted to come and stay at his house for the weekend. He pointed across the street, to a café, where his wife was sitting at a table on the footpath. She waved at me, and smiled. It was very strange, *agape*, but I almost felt as though I knew them. As though I had known them before.'

'Had you met them, do you think?'

'No, how could I have? We moved in very different circles,' he said, with a wry grimace.

'So you just went home with them?'

'I said "no". I wasn't stupid. Why would I trust them? But Paul was insistent. He asked if I wanted to just come and have dinner. I didn't have to go into their house, I could eat on the driveway, but they would feel better knowing I'd had a proper meal.'

'That's very kind of them.'

'They were kind.'

'Yes.'

'And that's it? You went for dinner and, what? Just stayed?'

'It wasn't that easy. I went for dinner, and ate on the driveway. They invited me in, I refused. They asked me to come back the next night, and I did.'

CLARE CONNELLY 149

'Why do you think they went to the trouble?'

'I asked him that, once. You know they could never have children of their own? And yet, they didn't adopt, they didn't foster. But he said that when he saw me, so skinny and hungry, he just felt like he'd been put on earth to take care of me.' His voice was gruff as the memory of that permeated his chest. 'They never pushed me. I never felt like they wanted anything in return for their generosity, except my safety. After about a month of dinners, I trusted them enough to stay. It was supposed to be for a weekend, but then Paul began to talk to me about his work, and it was like a fuse had been lit in my belly. For the first time, I felt all these neurons in my brain connecting, lighting up like a Christmas tree. I was obsessed with everything he said: the business, the opportunities. He saw it, and gave me a chance to work with him, on the basis that I went back to school. And so, there you have it. For the next three years, I went to school, worked with Paul, and ate Stephanie's food. I grew healthy again, nourished, and though they never asked me to say that I loved them, or to pay them back in any way, for the first time in my life, I had a bed, and I didn't fear that it would be taken away. They gave me the greatest gift I could have known. Security.'

He didn't realise she was crying until a tear thudded onto his chest. He brushed his thumb over her cheek, wiping her tears away.

'I didn't even cry, when they died,' he muttered, staring up at the ceiling, remembering the bleakness of that day. 'But it was like an anchor point in my life had been ripped away. I had briefly known what it was like to belong to a family, of sorts, and just like that, it disappeared.'

'Oh, Theo,' she murmured, pulling up higher so she could press a kiss to his lips, before resting her head on his shoulder. 'I'm so glad you met them, that they took you in.'

'As am I,' he agreed. It had been a perfect relationship for him—and for them. Neither had wanted something that the other wouldn't give. He knew that if they'd pushed him for more, he'd have run a mile, but they hadn't.

'I just remember you appearing, and yes, you were skinny,' she murmured. 'But you were also so vital, so...'

He tilted his face to look at her, and despite the seriousness of their conversation, a smile lifted his lips at the memory of the crush she'd had on him.

'Yes?'

She rolled her eyes. 'I'm not here to make your head any bigger.'

He grinned, his fingers drawing invisible patterns on her back. But they slowed, as his mind went back to that time, those first few years with the Georgiadeses. 'You were such a quiet kid,' he murmured. 'So withdrawn.'

'You made me nervous.'

He shook his head, though. 'It wasn't just around me. I saw you with your friends, your parents. You were always watching.'

She bit into her full lower lip, in a way that made his cock react instantly.

'I was always watching,' she admitted, several moments later, so he'd wondered if she was going to answer him at all. 'Or maybe it would be more accurate to say I was always anticipating.'

'Anticipating what?'

She sighed. 'Trigger points for my parents.'

'What does that mean?'

'Like, little things that people say, or do, that would tip them over the edge. Make them think of Mary when they weren't prepared.' She cleared her throat.

'You managed their grief.'

'Yes,' she admitted, huskily.

'Annie, you know it's not your job, don't you?'

She nodded, but frustration whipped his insides.

'Because you seem to still be caught up in this—in turning your life into an act of service. What else explains why you came to Sydney? Why you agreed to marry me?'

Her cheeks flushed and he let his hand drop to the mattress. Her eyes lifted to his, and he felt the weight of things she wasn't saying then, in a way that made him pull back. Because this was the kind of conversation he knew they were better avoiding. He didn't want to feel sorry for his wife; he didn't want to feel anything for her. And so he pulled his arm away from her and stepped out of bed, uncaring for his nakedness, just knowing he wanted to get away.

Despite what he'd said, sleeping together changed everything. Without discussing it, they no longer tried to keep one another at a physical distance. The moment he walked in the door, they reached for each other, coming together hard and fast, and then taking hours each night to explore and feel, to pleasure and be pleased by.

Working late was a thing of the past. Theo did his level best to stick out a full day, but by the early afternoon, all he could think about was getting home to his wife and sinking into her. The only reason he accepted this shift in their dynamic was the certainty he held that it was purely physical. There would be no more deep and meaningful conversations in bed, no more letting her get under his skin. This time, the partition for Annie would remain firmly locked in place—she would not take over his thoughts again, as she had five years ago, no matter what happened between them physically.

They made love in the pool, the spa, the shower, on the kitchen table, against walls, on the floor, in the car—wherever they were was no barrier. It was as though the floodgates had been unlocked and there was no going back. Or maybe it was because they knew they had a finite time for this, and they didn't want to waste it.

Without discussing it, they spent every minute they could in each other's arms, so when the night of her father's birthday rolled around, Annie found it almost impossible to think of going out without him. But what choice did she have? She particularly didn't want to risk things changing between her and Theo, going back to what they'd been like before. While they were hardly sharing each other's deepest, darkest secrets, there was an inherent intimacy to what they were doing, and the thought of losing that made her body feel weak with despair. In the back of her mind, she knew that wasn't without risk.

She knew that at some point, she'd have to walk away. The terms of their divorce were already agreed upon, after all, and she couldn't lose sight of that fact, no matter how good it felt to just be with him again. But for now, she wanted *this*.

'You look stunning,' he murmured, when she walked into the kitchen wearing a red dress with a low-cut neckline. 'If a little overdressed.' He indicated his own attire—just a pair of shorts.

Anxiety trembled inside of her—aware that she was on the brink of upsetting the apple cart and desperately wanting not to—but she pushed it aside. They'd come so far; she could be honest with him, without ruining the good thing they had going on. 'Actually, I'm going out,' she said. 'I have a dinner.'

His expression was immediately closed off to her—familiar, though she hadn't seen him react like that in a week and a half. 'I see.'

She could practically hear the questions forming inside his mind—questions she didn't want him to ask, because she didn't want to lie. 'I won't be late,' she said, hoping it would assuage whatever he was going to say, and strolling around to put a hand on his chest. 'Wait up for me?'

His eyes raked her face, a frown touching the corners of his lips, as he nodded once: a crisp, curt acknowledgement.

She let out a soft breath of relief then kissed him, her body immediately stirring to life. He pulled away though, his eyes distant. 'Have fun.'

Her chest hurt as though a bag of cement had been pressed against it. She turned away quickly, wishing, more than anything that she could stay here with him instead.

Her hand was on the door, when he caught up with her. 'You're not going to say where you're going?'

She closed her eyes against that, before turning to face him, lifting a hand to play with the diamond necklace she wore. 'A birthday party,' she said, after a beat.

He nodded thoughtfully. 'For a friend?'

Her eyes were hooked to his. She wished he hadn't asked. She shook her head, slowly.

'I see. Someone I know?'

'Theo—'

'You weren't going to tell me?'

'It's—'

'Your father's birthday.'

She pressed a hand to her brow, trying to think. 'How did you know?'

'Is it a secret?'

She bit into her lip. 'No, but—'

'I remember the date, Annie—it is a week before my foster mother's birthday,' he said, reminding her of that fact.

She swallowed past a constricted throat. 'I have to go—you don't.'

'He's my father-in-law,' Theo pointed out.

'Yes, but we both know how you feel about him.'

Silence sparked between them, the weight of what they were both feeling making it hard to wade through.

'Are you forgetting why I suggested this marriage, *agape*?' he asked, almost conversationally. 'The whole point was to show your father, at every opportunity, that he lost, and I won. That he was wrong about me—about us.'

She felt like her heart was undergoing a series of elec-

tric shocks as she shook her head. It was the truth, and yet
she wanted to argue against it, to deny it. That couldn't
really be at the heart of why he'd suggested this. Not
after the last week and a half. Not after how everything
had changed between them. Surely, that same angry hate
didn't still consume him?

'It's his birthday,' she said, weakly, as her mind tried
to keep up with this development.

'And?'

She pressed a hand to his chest, eyes imploring. 'Don't
do this, Theo.'

But his eyes were glittering with dark determination, and she barely recognised the man he'd become.
'I will be ready soon. Knowing your father, I presume
it's black tie?'

She closed her eyes on a wave of despair. 'Please,' she
said. 'Don't pick this fight.'

But when she blinked up at him, Theo was gone.

A stone seemed to drop, right through her body, landing hard in her gut.

She pressed her back against a wall, sucking in a deep
breath that hardly seemed to touch her lungs.

All Theo could do was stick to the plan. It was, as he'd
pointed out to Annie, the reason he'd proposed this marriage. The thought of throwing their relationship in the
face of the man who'd once told Theo that he was *pure
scum and always would be'*, was something he'd relished
the thought of.

As for Annie, she'd just have to cope with that.

And yet, glancing across at her, as the car slid through
the streets of Athens towards her family home, something

gnawed at the edges of his gut, as awful as the pervasive hunger he'd known as a child. Tension radiated from every line of her slim body. It was evident in the way she clasped her hands in her lap, the way she refused to look at him. He ached to do something to stir feelings in her, so she'd appear more like the wild, passionate, beautiful woman he'd been lusting after nonstop.

But sex—no matter how good—was just sex, and Annie was a woman he'd married as a means to an end. He owed himself this. Nothing could trump that—not even their chemistry.

So he sat in stony silence beside her, not reaching for her, not even to hold her hand.

There was no comfort he could give anyway, and he wouldn't pretend otherwise. For as long as his plan was to hurt her father, to make him eat crow, using Annie as a tool for that, he could hardly expect Annie not to mind.

As the car pulled to a halt in the busy driveway of their mansion, he did reach for her though, putting a hand on her knee and drawing her churning gaze to his face.

'I want you to remember two things, Annie,' he said, his voice heavy with loathing for the words he was about to speak. Hating himself then, even when he didn't dare question his commitment to this plan.

She was almost unrecognizable, with her pretty face so pale and pinched. 'Yes?' Her voice was barely a whisper.

He clenched his jaw, hesitating a moment, to draw strength.

'At the end of this marriage, your father will be a very rich man again. That's all you care about, remember?

That's why you came to me. You're getting what you wanted. What you agreed to.'

She fidgeted with her fingers so violently he had to fight an urge to reach out and clamp his hand over them.

'And the second?'

'We have a deal. You play your part, just like we agreed, or the arrangement's off.'

Her lips parted in surprise and whatever had been gnawing at his gut burst it apart completely. He put a hand on his door, opening it before he could take the words back, or at least apologise for what he was about to put her through.

Theodoros Leonidas didn't do regret, or uncertainty or compassion. He was stronger than steel, determined and ruthless. Those things had stood him in good stead—he wouldn't change now, not even for Annie.

CHAPTER ELEVEN

FROM THE MOMENT they walked into the party, Annie could feel the whispers. The speculation. And yes, the jealousy, from all the women who looked at Theo, saw his beauty and his wealth and wanted a piece of it, wondering how she, Annie Langley, had secured the hottest bachelor in Athens. Though their wedding had been widely publicized, and was well-known in these circles, this was only their second time out and about, in public together, and she fully expected her family's 'friends' to descend like hawks.

As for Theo, the change in his behaviour gave her whiplash. In the car, he'd been so calculated and businesslike, inflicting pain on her without appearing to care, so it had taken a monumental effort not to give in to the tears that she'd felt stinging behind her eyes.

Now, in the throng of the party, he was a study in attentive husbandry, one hand on the small of her back the whole time, his fingers stroking the base of her spine, his body so close to hers she could feel his warmth—even though it did little to thaw the ice in her heart.

'Darling,' her father's greeting, when they arrived,

encompassed her alone. He pressed a kiss to her cheek, then said, 'Thank you for coming.'

'We wouldn't have missed it for the world,' Theo responded, drawing Annie even closer to his side, and moving the hand from her back to her hip, possessively holding her to him. 'Would we, *erota mou*?' My passion.

The term of endearment was not one he'd used before, and though she might otherwise have liked it, the knowledge that he'd employed it purely to sting her father took any pleasure out of his huskily spoken words. As did the kiss he planted on the top of her head.

Elliot Langley did then look at Theo, and with such undisguised contempt Annie shivered. 'I wasn't aware you were coming.'

'My wife and I are inseparable,' Theo said, dropping any pretense of warmth. The words were, if anything, an arctic challenge. 'A wise man would know better than to try it.'

Annie glanced up at Theo, and opened her mouth to warn him, to scold him, anything, but the look he threw her held a warning, and she remembered what he'd said in the car. Any diversion from the role she was supposed to play, and the wedding would be off.

'A wiser man would know trying is unnecessary,' her dad surprised her by saying, but his own voice was just as frigid and unyielding as Theo's had been. 'You two have unfinished business, I can see that. But sooner or later, my daughter will realise that she can do so much better than this—Annie has a lot of potential to reach for, and a street kid from Athens isn't it.'

'Please, Daddy,' Annie said, her heart dropping to her toes, hating the words he was saying, hating the scene they were going to create if they didn't take care. 'Not now, not here.'

Elliot's lips were grim. 'You shouldn't have brought him.'

'Annie would not have come without me. Not knowing that I was unwelcome,' he said, and guilt flicked through her, because that's how she should have felt. Wasn't it? Knowing that her father had invited her, and not Theo. That he'd organised a big party and tried to exclude her husband. At the time, she'd been glad: she didn't want her father's birthday to ruin the status quo she and Theo had established. Except...

She looked up at Theo and now her heart sank for a different reason. She'd betrayed him, five years ago, by breaking up with him because her parents had insisted, but had tonight been another betrayal? Another failure to stand up for him, and do what was right? When had Theo ever had anyone in his corner?

If theirs had been a real marriage, she would have done just what he said. Come hell or high water, she would have stuck by him *this time*. But knowing that his sole objective was to pain her father, she'd been trying to do the right thing by everyone.

'Theo,' she said, softly, her words weakened by confusion. 'Let's go and get a drink. I'm parched.'

'The bar is by the pool,' Elliot muttered. 'Try not to fall in.' The last rejoinder was for Theo alone.

When they were at the bar, she looked up at her husband and said, 'I'd apologise for his behaviour, but I suspect you're delighted to have been able to goad him like that.'

Theo looked anything but delighted though, which

only made her feel worse. His dark eyes glinted with disapproval when they locked to hers. 'I'm starting to remember why I hate these people so much.'

'You're the darling of these people. I swear half of these women, at least, are staring daggers at me.'

'I will never be a darling to these people,' he contradicted swiftly, turning away from her to order their drinks—a scotch for himself and a champagne for Annie. 'They know as well as your father does—I don't belong.'

'I don't know why you have such a chip on your shoulder.'

He sent her a look that spoke volumes. 'Just as well. You do not need to know. You just need to act the part.' And to cement that, he dropped his mouth and claimed hers, in full view of anyone who cared to look their way. Pleasure ripped through her, but it was a heavy weight of intensity, too, a sadness and grief at the way he'd relegated anything she might feel, putting the focus purely on the physical. She didn't need to know anything too deep about him: it wasn't relevant. All he cared about was this newlywed act.

Knowing the kiss was for show, feeling the hurt of that lash through her, didn't change the effect it had on Annie. It didn't change the way her pulse went haywire and her whole body seemed to catch fire, so that she very quickly forgot where they were and fell against him, her whole self surrendered to him, and the pleasure he could dole out, whenever he wanted to.

He pulled back, looking down at her with a smile that didn't reach his eyes. 'You're an excellent actress, Annie. Perhaps you missed your true calling.'

And her heart, battered and splintered as it already

was, exploded into a billion tiny shards that would be, so far as she knew, impossible to stitch back together.

'Keep it up and I might have to think of a way to give you a bonus.'

'Go to hell,' she said, pasting a smile to her face even when she felt like sobbing. 'You really are a complete bastard.'

His eyes glinted and she could have sworn she saw relief on his face. 'Yes, I am. Don't forget it again.'

He knew the futility of hatred, yet he couldn't stem it. Or perhaps it was just that he was seeking refuge in it. Like the more time he spent with Annie, and the closer she got to pushing out of her little box again, the more Theo leaned into his anger. Anger was familiar. Anger was useful to him. Anger had never betrayed Theo.

Elliot Langley had torn shreds off Theo five years ago, unconsciously reviving every single stroke of pain Theo had been handed in his life, making him feel worthless, useless, as though he were a complete waste of skin. He'd hated the older man for a long time, but until Elliot took to the stage to thank his guests for coming, Theo hadn't fully grasped the extent of his hatred.

The thank-you speech started with an acknowledgement of how many people had shown up—and Theo had silently, cynically mused on the likelihood that the full guest list probably had something to do with the exceptional quality of the open bar, and the fact several journalists were circulating, taking photographs for to-morrow's papers. But then the speech had moved on, to pay tribute to those who couldn't be with him: his wife, and his daughter, Mary. He spoke for at least twenty minutes about the older sibling, and all the while, Annie stood at Theo's side, still like a statue, a polite smile frozen on her face. He listened to descriptions of Mary's prodigal piano playing, her kindness, how she'd brought such meaning to their lives, and he waited, and waited for anything of a similar ilk to be said about Annie.

Finally, at the end, he finished with, 'But at least, I still have Annie. My Annie.' Except, when his eyes had slid sideways to Theo, Elliot's lips had tightened in a dismissive line, and any further adoration he might have deigned to offer had been swallowed up by obvious disgust. 'Enjoy your night,' Elliot had concluded, to a round of polite applause.

Theo had turned to Annie, wanting to say something to placate her, to offer sympathy, or at least show that he understood, but Annie simply turned that ghoulish smile on him and said, 'I'm not in the mood, okay?'

'Annie—'

'Am I allowed to go to the bathroom on my own, or will you take that as some kind of failure in my play-acting?'

Now he knew what was twisting at his gut. Shame. It seemed to take over his whole body, and he hated the feeling. He didn't want to overthink it, to analyse why he felt like he'd followed a road he thought would lead to salvation and now instead suspected might pave the way to hell. He tightened his shoulders, tamping down on his self-doubt and said, voice calm, 'I'll be here.'

'And I'll be right back—' and then, for good measure, she added, with obvious disgust '—*erota mou*.'

Theo swallowed back whatever he'd been about to say in response, and the knowledge that he'd done something tonight he would never be able to undo, even if he wanted to.

He watched her walk through the guests, head held high, with the sense that once upon a time, practically another lifetime ago, he'd held something very, very precious in his hands, and he just hadn't known how to keep a hold of it. All this time he'd blamed her for breaking it off, for being weak under her parents' snobbish pressure, perhaps even for feeling as they did about him, but maybe the problem had been Theo all along.

Maybe he hadn't really understood her life.

Her pressures.

Her aching need to fix everything for everyone.

Maybe he'd been the one to let her down, by walking away without a backwards glance, too proud to push her to reconsider, refusing to beg and be rejected again. He'd gleaned how her parents had molded her, trying to turn Annie into Mary, trying to stem their grief with a perfect replacement, and he'd known how much of a toll that had taken on her. But until tonight, he hadn't really understood just how programmed she'd been—all her life—to do whatever her parents asked of her. To be the perfect daughter, even at the expense of her own happiness, and what a futile, unrewarding duty that was.

She'd tried to tell him when they'd shared lunch at the restaurant near the Acropolis, but even then, he'd let the conversation go rather than pushing her to expand. Because he hadn't wanted to know the truth? Because he'd been afraid of what it might mean for him if he started to see how hard Annie had had it, all her life? Had he avoided asking questions because he didn't want to be forced to question his actions in pushing her into this marriage? The realization that he was not so dissimilar to her parents, in expecting Annie to play a part for his benefit, sat in his gut like a stone.

But what good was there in raking over the embers of their past? He'd done what he'd done, as had she. They'd both made their choices, and now they had a marriage bed to lie in together. The past could not be changed—it was better to accept that owing to the past, they had no future. Even if he could get past what had happened all those years ago, Annie would never be able to forgive him for the way he'd blackmailed her into this. And after starting to understand her life better, he wasn't sure he'd be able to forgive himself, either.

She stared at her reflection for a long time, trying to pick out the familiarity of her features, to anchor herself to the core of who she was. What she believed. What she knew.

But it had been such a long time since Annie Langley had really thought about who *she* was and what *she* wanted. All her life, she'd been a daughter. A dutiful fill-in, needed to make their family somewhat full again.

From the moment Mary had died, Annie's purpose on earth had changed. She'd been content to live in Mary's shadow before, aware that her sister was a rare diamond, shining brighter than most other people. But after Mary had died, Annie had been rubbed and rubbed and rubbed by parents who were desperate to try to make her shine in all the same ways Mary had, never mind that Annie might have had her own ways of shining, if only she'd been allowed.

Distant memories of having, once upon a time, loved drawing and art—which had led to her wanting to own her own art gallery—flared to life in her chest. Her parents had shown no interest in her artistic talents, for that was not something Mary had shared. She remembered that she'd loved poetry, too, and had read all the romantics before her tenth birthday. But over the years, she'd morphed into a strange half human, exhibiting a performative role in the family, acting as she thought Mary might have. Then, when her mother died, Annie had taken on those roles in the house, too: organising social events, keeping in touch with their friends, overseeing the family business. She had tried to be everything to everyone to the extent she no longer recognised any part of her true self.

But back then, all those years ago, she'd felt like Theo understood and saw her. Even without talking deeply about her life, about any of this, he'd looked at Annie and seen *her*. She'd fallen in love with him, but she'd also fallen in love with the woman she'd been when he was around—because she could just be herself. For the first time in her life, she'd been with someone who didn't want anything of Annie except *her*. Her happiness, her thoughts, her pleasure.

But that version of Theo seemed a thousand light-years away from this reality. Which would hurt a lot less if she didn't feel so much for him. If she didn't look at him and experience a yawning ache to go back to what they were. And yet, even then, what they were now was somehow more real, more honest, warts and all. Was it better to be in a flawed relationship than a seemingly perfect one that didn't have depth—because he kept her at arm's length?

Or was it possible that she was blinded by feelings

that she really wished she didn't have. She'd gone into this swearing that she hated him, because of how he'd maneuvered her into this marriage, but when she glanced into her heart, it wasn't hate she saw. It was so much more complicated than that. But swirling at the depths of all her regret over the past was this one, shining kernel of truth—almost as bright as her enormous engagement ring—she loved him. She was in love with the husband who'd married her for revenge. And what kind of fool did that make her?

No matter how Annie felt, if he was determined to constantly bring them back to how this had started—in hatred and revenge—then there was no hope for them. Maybe she needed to take a page out of his book, and focus purely on protecting herself. Give Theo what he wanted: a public marriage, and nothing else behind closed doors.

She sniffed, pinching her cheeks to bring some colour back to them.

She hated it. She hated it so much, but what could Annie do? She'd agreed to this, and there was nothing left but to see it through. In the end, her father would have his company, but Annie might, at that point, hang up her acting shoes for good. It was time to find herself—away from the pressures of anyone else. It was time to stand on her own two feet. Or at least, it would be, when this marriage was over.

'I've made reservations for the Asteri tonight,' Annie murmured without looking up from her book the following morning. For his part, Theo was trying not to think about the fact they'd barely spoken since coming home from her father's party the night before, and for the first time in a long time, had also not touched.

He'd spent a deeply unsatisfying night staring up at the ceiling of his room, aware of his wife's soft rhythmic breathing, replaying every glance of hers, every word, every look that had indicated her hurt and sense of betrayal.

She'd played her part to perfection, of course. After coming back from the bathroom, she was impeccably attentive, standing at his side, making polite conversation, sipping champagne and acting as though she had not a care in the world. But it had been so fake, her act so brittle he felt as though one word from him might cause her to snap.

In the end, he'd ushered them out of there as quickly as possible, rather than subjecting her—or himself—to another moment of the tense estrangement.

'The Asteri?' he frowned, though he was familiar with the venue. It was one of *the* hotspots of Athens.

'You want our marriage to be public, right? Where better than somewhere like that,' she said, her voice blanked of emotion. Frustration zipped through him, but he couldn't name why. After all, she was right, but after last night, he wanted to make everything *less* public. He wanted to batten down the hatches here at home, keep her here, in his bed, until the Annie he'd glimpsed over the last week came back to him.

Except, the whole point of this was to rub their marriage in her father's face—to make him realise that the exact thing he'd forbidden from happening five years ago was now a reality. All Theo had to do was think back to that conversation, to the things the old man had said, and his resolution firmed. He just hadn't realised how much he'd hate making Annie collateral damage.

When he'd made this deal, he'd presumed he'd almost enjoy putting her through this, but for whatever reason, he had to admit to himself now that the opposite was true. She was hurting, and he wasn't enjoying that. He was hating it.

'Great,' he said, adopting the same, nonchalant tone, despite the turmoil of his thoughts. 'What time?'

'Nine o'clock.'

He nodded once, trying to think of something to say to fill the silence. An explanation or apology, but both died on his lips.

She glanced at him, though somehow he felt more as though she was looking through him. 'I'm going out—shopping. I'll be back before nine.'

He watched her leave, and told himself he was relieved. This version of Annie was like a knife being dragged over his flesh; she made him feel things he didn't want to face. Better to spend time apart than face that guilt front on, even if that made him a coward.

Five nights and five very public dates later, Theo had to admit—to himself at least—that he was at his wit's end. Annie had played the part of doting wife to perfection, but only for as long as they were in public. The minute they were collected by his driver, and nestled in the privacy of his car, the mask dropped, and she was back to icing him out, almost like she wished he didn't exist.

Except she didn't do anything quite so overt. She was still polite to him, speaking if he asked questions, offering cool smiles, and she still slept in their bed, albeit huddled to one side of it. But she'd pulled a shield over herself, and no matter what he said or did, he couldn't crack through it.

Worse than having her break up with him because her parents had demanded it was this: living alongside her quiet, brutal contempt. Knowing that she was choosing to ice him out, not because her parents didn't see any value in him, but because *she* didn't. He was in freefall, and all of his usual anchor points were insufficient to stop it. Just looking at her made the whole world lose its shape.

The following night, when Annie announced yet another public engagement—this time, the opening of a restaurant followed by drinks at the pier—he'd almost snapped at her that he was sick of being dragged around town for the sake of photographers before remembering that it had been *his* requirement, not hers. She was simply living up to it.

When she appeared in the living room in yet another stunning dress that showed way too much skin, he ground his teeth together and tried to ignore how much he wished they were just staying home.

They'd made their point. Their photograph had been splashed over the tabloids. Everyone knew about their marriage.

'Can you be bothered going out again?'

'I wasn't aware I had a choice.'

His gut felt like it had been washed in acid. 'Don't say that.'

She tilted her chin, glaring at him. 'I'm doing what you asked of me. If you've changed your mind, fine. I'm just as happy to stay in.'

But she wasn't happy. Annie was anything but, and it was all because of him. He ignored the pain in his chest,

the feeling of something beautiful being tarnished forever. 'No, you've made the reservation. We'll go out.'
At least when they were out, she pretended to like him.
Here, at home, he couldn't escape her silent judgement,
and it was eating him alive.

'Great,' she smiled, over-bright and clearly false. 'I'm
ready when you are.'

The restaurant was in an industrial part of the city that
had gradually become a haven for exclusive bars and
clubs, though Theo couldn't for the life of him say why.
He presumed it had started as some kind of ironic joke,
but now some of the most exclusive haunts in the city
were in between abattoirs and box factories.

He couldn't fault the decor of the restaurant though,
nor the menu. He sat opposite his wife and made the
obligatory small talk, admiring the way she volleyed it
back, as though she wasn't hating him the whole time.
They were interrupted often, by people he knew, or she
knew, or sometimes, people who knew them both, and
for Theo's part, he was as equally glad for the interrup-
tion as he was resentful of it.

It gave him a momentary reprieve, while also allowing him to watch her at work. To watch the way she as-
sumed a role so easily—not because he'd asked her to,
this time, but because he suspected she'd been doing it
all her life. Being who she was expected to be. Playing a
part. Being Mary. Then her mother. Being whatever was
needed of her, always putting other people first, always
being what was needed, not what she wanted.

Had that been true of her then, too? Had she been

that way with him—playing the role of what she believed he wanted?

He'd thought not. He would have sworn the Annie
he'd spent time with was true to herself, to the woman
she wanted to be, but how could he know? She'd been
so perfect for him, their time together so—right—but
maybe that was down to her acting skills?

As Annie spoke to the two women who'd approached
their table, Theo looked at her without really seeing. No,
he was back in time, in the water at the island, making
love to his wife in a way that was totally real, without
pretense, without make-believe. That had been an act of
total honesty—his need, her need, raw desperation and
hunger, bringing them together, bonding them in a way
he'd resented at the time, because it had been her first
sexual experience. Now he felt so differently about that.

Everything felt flipped on its head, and he hated it.
He wanted to see the real Annie again, to strip her back
to the essence of who she was, before this play-acting
had come into the equation.

The waiter appeared to clear their plates, and the
women dispersed with a manicured wave in Annie's direction, which Theo barely noticed.

'Let's go back to the island.' And until he heard himself say it, he hadn't even been aware he was going to
suggest it.

For a second—barely even a second, in fact—her
mask slipped, and she looked at him like he'd sprouted
two heads.

'Why?'

Great question. But now that he'd made the suggestion, he found himself wanting to see it through. He

leaned forward, an intensity in his gaze, as if he could make her understand if he just looked hard enough. 'To get away from this.'

Annie compressed her lips in a gesture he was intimately familiar with: contemplation. She was trying to make sense of his statement. '*This* is what you wanted.'

And she was right. This had indeed been what he'd originally envisaged, back in Sydney, when she'd come to him for help. And he'd responded by blackmailing her. His chest seemed to compress, as though a cement truck had dropped its entire load on him. So much had changed since then, not least of all his certainty that this revenge plan was wise. 'Now I want the island.'

Her lips pressed together again, harder, so her mouth was white-rimmed, and her eyes showed something a lot like panic. 'I don't think it's a good idea.'

'Are you saying no?'

'Am I allowed to say no?'

That cut right through him, and he felt almost as though he couldn't breathe, as though he were drowning. The last thing he wanted was for her to feel trapped. 'Annie…' He leaned forward. 'No one forced you into this. No one is forcing you to stay.'

Desperation contorted her features. 'Really? If I asked to leave, wouldn't you just point out that we have an agreement?'

He hated that she was right. He hated that she evidently felt trapped. But most of all, he hated the fact that if he were to invoke their agreement to get her to stay, he knew now that it had less to do with the terms they'd reached and more to do with him just wanting her in his life a bit longer. Acknowledging that to himself was like leaping off the edge of a building. It was a warning, and in an instant, his whole mindset shifted. They couldn't go back to the island. They couldn't do anything that would strip away their barriers, and draw them closer together. He refused to weaken where Annie was concerned. Never again.

'Are you saying you want to leave?' His voice was grim, and already he was preparing for the reality of that. She'd walked away from him once, and he'd known she'd do it again. Was he really surprised?

'Please, let's not do this here.' She smiled tightly, for the sake of the audience, but he couldn't wipe the stern insistence from his own features. 'We still have the bar to go to,' she reminded him. 'I don't want to fight.'

'I'm not fighting.'

'Nor am I.'

'You're implying that you don't have any autonomy in this marriage. That's not true.' He had to hear her deny it. He had to hear her agree that she'd walked into this with her eyes open.

She pulled a face. 'I told you, not now.'

And the fact she couldn't give him the reassurance he suddenly needed was like a storm cloud breaking over his world. Everything seemed different, seen through that lens. 'Then let's go home. I'm not in the mood to preen around in some bar so we can get our photo taken.'

She flinched. 'I thought that's exactly what you wanted.'

'No. All of Athens knows we're married, including your father. Job done. Let's go.' He scraped his chair back abruptly, dropping some money onto the table and holding out a hand to her. She stared at it for a long time and his heart dropped at what he felt to be yet another rejection: not touching him.

'Annie.' His voice was meant to be a plea, but he supposed it could also have sounded vaguely like a warning, if she was intent on seeing him as some kind of monster—and why wouldn't she? Her fingers trembled when she put them in his palm. He closed his own around them, in an effort to bring stillness, and when she got to her feet, he pulled her close to his body. 'We need to talk.'

He didn't know what he'd say, but with every single fibre of his intuition, he knew this was no way to live— even for eighteen months. He was not going to subject her to it, not for all the revenge, or all the money, in the world. Even when he desperately wanted her to stay, it wouldn't be like this. It couldn't be.

CHAPTER TWELVE

ANNIE'S NERVES WERE stretched almost to the breaking point. She'd spent the last week acting her little ass off, hoping to provoke him into a reaction. Hoping to provoke him into saying or doing *something* that showed he *felt* anything. Anything other than a soul-destroying need for vengeance, at least. Anything other than hatred for her father.

And tonight, she'd seen that, but she had no idea what he was feeling, and the not knowing was making her stomach twist into billions of tangly knots. They drove home in silence, like the calm before the storm, she'd presumed. But even once they walked inside his luxurious mansion, he was still lost in thought.

So much for talking.

She went to their room and took a long shower, scrubbing her body with a loofah, hoping to bring about a sense of calm. Or if not calm, at least familiarity. But everything was all twisty and knotty and so by the time she stepped out of the shower and wrapped a towel around herself, and walked into the bedroom to find Theo just unfastening the top button of his shirt, something inside of her snapped.

'I thought you wanted to talk,' she said, uncaring of the fact she was all but naked.

He turned to face her slowly, a look on his face she'd never seen before. 'We need to,' he agreed, but his tone was grim, and she had a feeling a lead balloon had been dropped right on top of her.

Or an executioner's axe was about to fall.

She stared at him, waiting, her heart thudding against her ribs.

'This isn't working.'

'Really?' Her voice came out strangled. 'Because if you wanted to upset my father, I'd say you've done an excellent job.'

His eyes narrowed a little and his lips flattened. 'That is what I wanted. I thought it was what I wanted more than anything, but it turns out, the price was too high.'

'Price?'

'I can't do this.' He cleared his throat. 'I won't do this. To you, Annie. I won't do this to you.'

Her heart stammered now, fast and irregular. What was he saying? 'It's already done. We're married. We have a contract.'

'That doesn't mean anything.'

Her jaw dropped. 'I don't understand.'

'We can change the contract.'

She felt weak enough to pass out. She'd wanted to goad him into a response, but she'd never thought it would be this. 'Is that what you want?'

His eyes closed, and when he spoke, his voice was low and gruff, loaded with accusation. 'What I want is to have never met you.'

'How can you say that?' she whispered, staring at

him across the room, body trembling. It hurt so badly, she had to lift a hand and press it to her chest, to stop her heart from splintering through her skin. 'What have I ever done to you, Theo? What have I ever done to deserve that?'

A muscle jerked in his jaw, but she was too angry now, too angry to even think about what she was saying. The words just tumbled out of her, drawn by emotion. 'All I have ever done, from the moment we met, is love you,' she shouted. 'I have loved you since I was eleven years old. I loved you when I was thirteen, fifteen, eighteen and begged you to kiss me—'

'On a dare,' he interrupted.

'Yes, they dared me to do it, but that's not why I asked. I wanted you to kiss me. I wanted you. Just like when I was twenty-one and begged you again. I have loved you always—'

'You walked away from me.'

'But I never stopped loving you,' she roared, shaking all over. 'I loved you even when I came to you in Sydney. When you suggested this marriage, I knew, deep down, that for me, it was something I actually wanted, because of how I felt about you. I couldn't admit it to myself, not when you were so angry with my father, but every single day, I have come to understand my heart, and now, I see it. I love you. And yet you stand there and tell me I am the bane of your life?' Tears ran down her cheeks but she refused to wipe them away, to say anything to him.

'I never asked you to love me,' he responded, his voice the opposite of hers—cold and calm.

'You didn't have to ask. That's not how it works.'

'I never *wanted* you to love me,' he said instead.

'Then what the hell were we doing back then, Theo? I fought with my parents over you, I fought for you. My mother had a heart attack in the middle of one of those fights. But I fought with them because I thought… I thought you loved me, too.'

He turned his back on her, his shoulders moving with the force of his breath.

'You told me I was special.'

He whirled back to face her. 'You are special. That has nothing to do with whether or not I love you, or want to be loved by you. We never had a future.'

Her jaw dropped and her knees felt impossibly weak. She moved to the edge of the bed and sat down, her knees no longer able to support her.

'I thought you understood,' he said, darkly. 'And I thought we could play this game without either of us getting hurt. But I am hurting you, every day of this marriage, and knowing that is cutting me to pieces. I do not want to live like this.'

She blinked across at him, her heart shifting in her chest. 'Cutting you to pieces?'

'I'm not a total bastard, Annie. I don't want you to suffer. Not because of me.' He frowned. 'Not because of anyone. I want you to be happy—I've always wanted that. Don't you get it? That's why I wish I'd never met you—I'm ashamed of what I've become. Ashamed of who I am to you.'

'Are you hearing yourself?' she demanded, standing up again and pacing across to him. 'You hate seeing me upset, you want me to be happy. Yet you think you don't feel something for me? You think you don't love me?'

His eyes swept shut.

'Do you really think you suggested this marriage just to get back at my dad? Or is it that deep down, it's what you really want, too, but don't want to admit to yourself?'

His jaw shifted as he ground his teeth. 'I've never wanted marriage.'

'You haven't let yourself want it,' she corrected. 'You were bounced from pillar to post as a child. Nobody loved you. You never knew security until you came to live with the Georgiadeses, then they died, too. And even now, a grown man of thirty-one, you're terrified to let yourself reach for happiness, in case it goes away again.' She bit back a sob. 'I understand that, Theo. I don't think anyone who's lived through what you have would feel differently. But at least take a second to think about what's in here.' She pressed a hand to his chest. 'Think about why it hurts you so much to see me hurting. Think about why you have been so angry at my father, for such a long time. Think about how it feels when we're together, why your first thought when I came to you for help was to lock me into this marriage, and ask yourself if that's really something you want to let go.'

'How it feels when we are together is like I'm holding a stick of dynamite, likely to go off at any moment, without warning.'

She frowned, not understanding the analogy.

'I don't know when this is going to end, but I know it will. All things do. Whether because you leave me, or your father makes you leave me, or because one of us dies, nothing lasts forever. I would rather control that, and I think it's best for you, too.'

'Don't you dare be such a paternalistic jackass. I don't need you deciding what's best for me. If you want me to move out, I will, but you should know that's *your* decision, not mine.'

'What do you want, then, Annie? Do you want to stay here, living with me, like this, for another seventeen months of this godawful marriage?'

She flinched. 'No. I want to stay living with you forever, in a wonderful, happy marriage, where we stop fighting everything we feel and accept that when I was eleven and you were fifteen, we met the loves of our lives, and our fate was sealed. I want you to accept that sex with us is never—and could never be—just sex. That every time we're together it's meaningful and beautiful, and special. I want you to know that I will always be here for you, that you can relax with me—'

'How can I after what happened last time?'

'Are you hearing yourself? You're making no sense. Two minutes ago, you told me that you never thought we were going to last. So why did it matter that I left you?'

'It's *why* you left me.'

'Because I love my parents?' she demanded. 'Because I have spent a lifetime playing the part of a stabilizer to them, and I didn't know how to stop? You think you're the only one who learned from that experience? I love my father, and I want him to be happy, but it's time for me to live my life, regardless of what he thinks and wants. And I choose you. I want you.'

A muscle jerked in his jaw. 'This isn't what I want.'

'Well, I don't believe you,' she said, moving to the wardrobe and removing her nightgown. She dressed quickly, staring at him the whole time, hating that even in that moment, she could feel heat and need building inside of her.

'This was a mistake.'

'How we got married, yes. But not that we are.' She put a hand on her hip. 'I'm not leaving you, Theo. If you really want me out of your life, you have to leave me. Divorce me. Announce it in the papers. Do whatever you have to do, but it needs to come from you. I'm not going to walk away from you again.'

'There's nothing to walk away from,' he muttered. 'This isn't a relationship.'

She rolled her eyes. 'You are completely delusional.'

'Annie.' He raised his voice. 'Listen to me. Our marriage is over. I don't want this. I don't want you. I made a mistake, and now I'm fixing it.'

Each word landed against her with a heavy thud. She shook her head, needing to clear those words, needing not to hear them, but he just stared at her, no hint of doubt on his face.

'I'll go to a hotel for a few days, while I find somewhere else to live. You stay here. I will uphold everything I agreed to in our deal, naturally. I'll fix your father's company, and then return it to you. I'm sorry I used you like this. I will always regret it.'

'Used me,' she whispered, shaking her head. 'Is that really what this was to you? Was I honestly just a means to an end?'

He closed his eyes at the accusation in her voice, but then, he was stuffing things into a bag and Annie was staring at him with the realization that he was actually about to walk out of his own home.

'Don't,' she shouted, eyes filling with tears. 'Don't you dare pack that bag. If either of us is leaving, it will be me. This is your home. I'm not staying in it without you.'

'You can leave, if you want, but either way, I'm going.'

'Does it mean nothing to you to hear that I love you?'

'It means I was even more careless than I thought. All I can hope is that you are mistaken.'

'I'm not,' she said. 'I love you. You need to look at me, and accept that. Accept that you are walking away from someone who has given you their heart, for always and ever. And Theo? That means something.'

He was silent.

'Coward. You're running away from me because you're terrified to love, knowing there's a risk that you'll lose me. So what? Aren't I worth taking that risk for? Don't we deserve a chance?'

His response was to walk out the door.

Theo went to the island, rather than a hotel, and that was a mistake, because memories of Annie chased him there. Even in the ocean, there was no solace. Whatever their first time had been about, it had imprinted on him in a way he couldn't shake. She was in the wind, the sand, the sky, the very air he breathed.

He stayed for a week, each day, hoping to wake up and feel something like his normal self, but without success.

On the eighth day, he returned to Athens with a heaviness in his gut he couldn't shift.

He thought about going home, but he couldn't. He didn't want to see Annie. He wished this whole thing had never happened. He'd been so focused on the chance for revenge against her father, he hadn't stopped to think about what that revenge might do to Annie. He hadn't stopped to think about the fact he was making her collateral damage, nor the fact that he really, really cared about that.

And even though he knew he couldn't be with her, he also knew he couldn't be responsible for ruining her life—and her relationship with her father.

She'd called him a coward? Maybe she was right. But he was going to stand up and fix at least one part of this debacle, starting with her father.

Nine days after walking away from Annie, he arrived at her father's house, grim-faced but determined, and pressed the doorbell.

A maid answered after a few moments.

'Is Elliot Langley in?'

'May I take your name?'

Theo compressed his jaw. 'His son-in-law.'

Even then, when'd come to relieve himself of the burdens of guilt and hate, he found it hard to step back from what he was feeling.

'Very good, sir. Please, come in. Mr Langley is in his study.'

Theo nodded once, but having only come to the house on the occasion of Elliot's recent birthday, he had no idea where that was. That must have shown on his features, because the maid said, 'Please, follow me.'

Theo strode behind her, noting the lack of photographs of Annie on the walls, whereas everywhere he looked there were pictures of his late daughter, Mary.

He knew what the dynamic had been, because Annie had told him, back then, but that didn't make it any harder to see. To imagine how it had been for Annie, growing up here, amongst this museum—a tribute to the little girl they'd lost. A little girl she could never replace, no matter how much her parents wanted her to.

Something cavernous opened up in his chest as Annie's spirit flooded through him. Annie, who'd never really been loved, either. Who'd only been wanted to stem the tide of grief, and hadn't been enough for that. Annie who had learned her role in life was to give up everything to please her parents, including her own independence, her own desires. Including him, even when he was what she'd wanted most.

Annie who'd come to him for help, and received instead the weight of Theo's bitter resentment and anger, who'd been destroyed by him when she'd most needed compassion.

The gnawing, cavernous hollow in the middle of his being expanded out. Regret was a third footfall, right behind him, chasing him relentlessly.

'Leonidas.' Elliot pushed back his chair, staring across his office at Theo, as though he'd seen a ghost. 'What the hell are you doing here?'

'We need to talk,' he said, striving to infuse his voice with a hint of cordiality, and failing.

'What the hell for? I thought I made it clear the other night—you're not welcome in my house.'

'Even as your son-in-law?' he asked, his lips sneering, before remembering he'd come here to be honest, to at least fix things, as much as he could, for Annie.

'The fact she was stupid enough to marry you doesn't change a thing about how I feel. She'll wake up and see the light one day.'

'And if she doesn't?'

'It's inevitable. You're not right for her. How could you ever hope to be? Someone like you…'

Theo crossed to the window and stared out at the familiar view of Athens. His own outlook, from his bedroom in the Georgiadeses' house next door, had been in this direction.

'It's good to see your elitist streak hasn't mellowed with age.'

'Is it elitist to speak the truth?'

'Your truth is exactly that—yours. Not mine, not Annie's. Never Annie's.'

'You were a mistake. You were always a mistake. She'll see that eventually.'

'Yes.' Theo dropped his head forward, the words piercing his soul. 'Our marriage was a mistake, you're right. My mistake, not hers.' The weight on his chest grew heavier. 'Annie married for love. I married for revenge.' He turned then, dark eyes glittering with ruthless anger, and saw the way Elliot had to brace himself against the desk. 'She married out of a love for you, and, I believe now, a love for me. Perhaps she hoped she could love us both enough to get beyond how much hatred you and I share for one another. One thing has become very clear to me, though. Our marriage will destroy her. Loving me will destroy her. You were right about that.'

'What do you mean, you married for revenge?'

Theo hesitated for the briefest moment, before forcing himself to admit what he'd come here to say. 'Annie needed my help with a professional matter. I gave it on the condition of this marriage.'

Elliot cursed loudly. 'You blackmailed my daughter?'

'Yes.' What was the sense in hiding it?

'For what possible reason?'

Theo compressed his lips.

'To get back at me,' Elliot groaned. 'Because I made her leave you back then. Are you really so petty and broken, that you cannot let bygones be bygones? Are you so damaged that you couldn't see Annie would be the one you hurt with this? Annie, who stood up for you until she was blue in the face. Annie would probably have walked out of her home for good that night, rather than lose you, if it hadn't been for her mother.'

Theo absorbed those charges with no small measure of hurt.

But Elliot was not finished. Face puce with anger, he shouted, 'Good Lord, what in God's name have you done?'

'Done?' Theo ground his jaw. 'I've let her go, Elliot. Just like you wanted me to. She's free. Annie and I will be getting divorced. It turns out, you win, after all.'

Elliot sat down in the chair behind his desk, staring at the wall opposite. 'You really are a fool, Leonidas.'

Theo made a scoffing noise of surprise.

'I never thought much of you, but at least you showed yourself to have good judgement. Are you telling me you've ended things with my daughter? *You've* broken up with *her*?'

A muscle jerked in his jaw as he heard the older man's shock. Hell, he could even understand the reasoning for it. What man in his right mind would walk away from Annie without a gun to his head? Even then...

'If you've hurt her—' Elliot said, the words ringing through the room.

Theo paced to the desk and pressed his fingertips

against the inlaid leather surface. 'Isn't that a little like the pot calling the kettle black?'

'What the devil does that mean?'

'Annie came to me hurt. She came to me broken. Because of you. Because of how you treated her—because of how you pushed her, her whole life, into Mary's shadow.'

The older man paled immediately, his lined face showing surprise and indignation, as well as something else. Something like guilt. 'You don't know what you're talking about.'

'I know that woman deserved better than to feel like a substitute for someone you loved more.'

'*I* love my daughter.'

'Perhaps. But loving someone doesn't always go hand in hand with treating them well.' The words fell like stones against him, thudding into the emptiness of his chest cavity in a way that he knew would leave permanent scars.

'I have always protected her, and tried to do what was right for her—'

'You've done what was right for you. You've spent your life trying to turn Annie into the person you thought she should become, rather than appreciate the woman she is.'

'This is none of your business.'

Theo opened his mouth to dispute that, to say that anything that concerned Annie would always concern him, but that would have been a lie, wouldn't it? Annie was not his wife in anything but name, and even that would soon be dissolved.

'If you've hurt her, Theo, so help me God—'

He narrowed his gaze, his gut rolling with acid waves. 'I would *never* hurt her.'

'Then where is she?' Elliot asked, eyes narrowed. 'I haven't heard from her since my birthday party. I could tell she was annoyed with me, but she would usually have called me by now.' The older man stood, then. 'Where is my daughter? Where is my Annie?'

Theo flinched then, because the sound in Elliot's voice was unmistakably worry, and yes, love. It might have been a love that was warped and shaped by his grief, but that didn't make it any less valid or sincere. Even though he hadn't been able to be the kind of father Annie wanted or deserved, that didn't mean he wasn't feeling concern for her now. He was a lot like Theo in that regard. They were married, and yet, Theo had been far from the kind of husband Annie had wanted or deserved. She'd loved him, and he hadn't been able to love her back. He hadn't been brave enough to let himself.

Ironically, he'd called her a coward at the beginning of their relationship, but if he forced himself to regard their relationship with honesty, wasn't it *he* who was afraid? He who was running? Heat flushed his skin.

'She's at my house,' he said, his chest cleaving apart to imagine her there. 'I told her she could live there as long as she wants, and I meant it.'

'Take me to her,' Elliot said, standing up. 'I want her home, here, with me.' He strode towards Theo then, his eyes laced with fury. 'You never were good enough to even breathe the same air as her, much less touch her. But then, you came back, and married her, and a part of me actually thought maybe you understood how special she is? Maybe you saw it? But you don't even love her, do you? You just did this to get back at me. And yet you can stand there, telling me I don't value my daughter for who she really is. You're a hypocrite, Theo.'

Theo wanted to say something to contradict that, to explain the complexity of his thoughts, to point out that many things could be true at once, but the words were strangled in his throat. All he could do was stare at the other man, his face an unknowing study in tortured contemplation.

Elliot, though, apparently didn't notice the turbulent ruminations going on inside Theo. 'How dare you? How bloody dare you? Take me to my daughter and then get the hell out of our lives, once and for all. She needs to get over you, you bastard.'

On that score, at least, they were in agreement.

Theo collapsed on the sofa, staring between his feet, his heart thudding heavily in his chest. There was no way of knowing when the note had been left, but a quick perusal of his security system showed that Annie had left the house an hour after him, the night they'd fought. The night he'd told her he didn't love her.

The night he told her their marriage was over.

He'd watched the grainy night-vision footage of her pulling a small suitcase down the steps and hailing a cab, and felt like his insides had been acid washed. By then, he'd been at the airport, about to take off for the island where he'd tried to forget about Annie, but all the while imagining her in his home, consoling himself that at least he could picture her going about her life there. That at least he'd given her that.

And now he had no idea where she'd gone.

Elliot had left the house, furious and scathing, blustering about filing a police report and Theo should consider the matter closed, seeing as he clearly didn't care for Annie anyway. Theo had wanted to shout at the older man to shut up, to stop saying things like that, but how could he deny it? If he'd cared for Annie, she'd have still been here. She'd have been safe in his house, safe with him, instead of God knew where.

He pushed up from his sofa, his heart thumping in his empty chest, as he paced the living room and tried to think. To imagine where she might go, where she could be living, who she'd be with. Friends? None that she was close to. She'd rarely travelled outside of Athens; as far as he knew there was nowhere she wanted to be, nowhere that called to her. Or if there was, he didn't know it. He didn't know where she'd turn to, in a dark moment of her life, and that gap in his knowledge physically hurt him. Suddenly, the idea that Annie was alive and he didn't know something so vital about her, didn't understand her well enough to know where she would flee to, was an impossible reality.

He couldn't live with it. He had to find her.

Theo reached for his phone and tried calling Annie. Again, and again, with no response. Then, with a sense of dread, he finally accepted that it was time to call the police himself, never mind that Elliot had already done so. He filed his own missing persons report, then he called a private security firm and enlisted their help, too. But even then, he just couldn't sit in his home, waiting for news. He had to do something, and so he went out on foot, scouring the city he knew so well, courtesy of having grown up in the back streets. He went to the restaurants they'd eaten at, the bars, hoping that he'd catch a glimpse of her, somewhere.

Anywhere.

Annie had barely left bed since checking herself into her hotel room. She couldn't say why she'd come back to it except that it had been the only thing she could think of, that awful night, when he'd ended their marriage. As though she could close this chapter of their lives just by coming back to where it had begun.

It hadn't worked.

The chapter was open. The wound, too, weeping and ghastly, so she'd climbed into bed and curled up in the fetal position, eyes squeezed shut. It hadn't helped to stem the tears, though. They'd fallen hard, almost saturating the pillow, but she'd just rolled over, onto the other side of the bed, and kept crying.

It was the most awful, heavy feeling, to finally have accepted how much she still loved Theo, and also accepting that he would never let himself feel that for her. Even if he did, in fact, love her, he wouldn't admit it, and he wouldn't act on it. It was futile and desperate.

Somewhere along the way, Annie lost track of the date. She eventually began to feel closer to human, to move from the bed to the small armchair and stare out at the city. To order room service that she would pick around the edges of, if not fully eat. At one point, she contemplated turning her phone on, but decided against it.

She didn't really expect to hear from Theo, but at the same time, it was possible he might reach out to her. Perhaps when he realised she was no longer at the house they'd shared? He'd no doubt be relieved she'd left quietly, without trying to revive their conversation. He'd finally pushed her away, and this time, it would be for good.

But the thought of her life, spanning before her without Theo in it, was its own form of torture. Annie's heart almost couldn't take it.

She moved back to the bed and curled beneath the covers, tears welling in her throat as she tried not to think about Theo: wanting him, needing him to reach for her and knowing he never would.

CHAPTER THIRTEEN

THE ROOM SERVICE came a little earlier than she'd expected, then again, she'd lost track of days and nights. It might have been a quiet Monday, for all she knew. She pushed out of bed, her limbs feeling heavy, and made her way down the carpeted corridor to the front door of her hotel room, pulling it inwards without noticing that the usual 'room service' announcement hadn't been made.

And stumbled backwards at the sight of Theo on the other side of the door, his face a mask of barely contained darkness. Anger? Fury? Worry? What? She didn't know. Only he was staring at her with those glittering eyes, his jaw clenched so tight it was practically squared off.

'Do you have any idea how worried we've been?' he demanded, striding through the open door and putting his hands on her forearms, holding her still so he could stare down at her face, as though needing to reassure himself that she was in fact standing right in front of him, alive and well.

Annie shook her head, shaking all over, unable to find any words.

'You disappeared, Annie. You disappeared. We had no idea where you were.'

She pulled away from him then. Moments earlier,

she'd been facing the reality of how desperate she was to be held by him, to feel his strength one last time, but now, it was the cruellest thing, because it meant nothing.

'I'm fine,' she lied, moving into the hotel room and looking around with a grimace. At least it looked tidy—she'd barely unpacked, much less touched anything besides the bed.

'You look—'

She didn't want to think about how she looked. She whirled around, trying to cling to anger instead of the spasming pain inside of her. 'I wasn't exactly expecting company or I might have gone to a little more effort.'

'Annie,' he groaned, and he dropped his head, pressing his hands to his face, so she stopped whatever tirade she'd been about to dredge up and looked at him properly. Saw his stance for what it was—desperation. Misery. Relief.

With legs that were shaking, she moved to the bed and sat down, needing the support.

'I have spent the last week imagining you—I don't know. I had no clue. It was only that your father remembered an old credit card, thought you might have been using that, that led to you being discovered.'

Her stomach dropped. 'My father? Tell me he doesn't know about any of this.'

Theo strode towards her, crouching between her legs. 'Why did you run away, Annie? Why did you try to hide from me?'

'I didn't run away,' she said, hollow. 'You ended our marriage, I simply left, as I said I would.'

'But you didn't use normal bank accounts. You have been hiding here.'

'I have been taking some time,' she said, sniffling. 'And why is this your business? You made it very clear that you didn't want any part of this marriage.'

'Yes, I did,' he said, a muscle jerking in his jaw. 'And do you have any fucking idea how much I have wanted to take those words back ever since? How much I have wanted to fix what I broke? How much I have needed to see you to make this right?'

She sucked in an uneven breath.

'Annie, you were right. Everything you said was right. When I met Paul Georgiades, it felt like I knew him before, like I had no choice but to go with him, to keep going back to him, but it was never really about Paul and Stephanie, as much as I respected and cared for them. It was always about finding my way to you. My other half. My beautiful, perfect other half, my reason for being, my reason for everything.'

She shook her head then, tears slipping down her cheeks, landing heavily on her thighs.

'I spent a long awful week on the island, and you were there, in my bloodstream, whispering your love to me, making me wake up and realise what I wanted. And then, I knew I had to fix this. I had to start by facing up to my hatred for your father, by trying to fix that, because you cannot live in a marriage where your husband and your father are sworn enemies.'

She sucked in another breath, the sound a wrenching half sob.

'How did you try to fix it?'

'By admitting the truth to him. But a strange thing happened. In telling him what I thought was the truth, I realised I'd been wrong all along. All I wanted, from the minute you walked into my life, was to keep you right here, with me, where you belong. I made it sound like it was about revenge, when in reality, it's always been this. It's always been you.

'When we were seeing each other, before, I felt as though I had been given the greatest gift known to man. Losing you was agony. I suppose I have been trying to insulate myself from that risk, to handle this on my terms, but I've been so wrong. So wrong. Even now, I stand before you begging you to come home to me, to tell me I'm not too late, that you can still love me after what I've done, when there is a huge part of me that wants to let you go, because I don't deserve you. Because I could never deserve you.'

'You've always had to protect yourself, Theo. I know that.'

'Yes, but that's no excuse.'

'Isn't it?' She caught his face with both hands. 'I don't need you to be perfect, Theo. I don't need you to get it right all the time. I didn't.'

'You?'

'Do you think you're the only one with regrets? Breaking up with you was the worst decision I ever made. I know why I did it. At twenty-two, with my mother in hospital having suffered a heart attack, I was desperate to fix everything. That's how I'd been raised. But I was young, and I didn't understand the ramifications of that decision. It's not one I would make now.'

'You were acting out of love for your family. Your decision was born of decency and goodness, of caring for someone else. Mine was purely selfish.'

'You've been through more than one person should

ever have to in a lifetime, Theo. It's okay to want to take care of yourself.'

'Please, don't be so forgiving. I deserve to feel this guilt.'

She laughed softly then, and the sound was such a surprise to her, that her heart seemed to bubble in answer. 'Theo, do you love me?'

He answered immediately. 'With absolutely the entirety of my heart.'

'Then can you do something for me?'

He hesitated longer then, though. 'Yes. Anything.' The second word was said with more conviction, and she knew he meant it. She knew that if she asked him to walk away, he would. But Annie had no intention of doing that.

'Would you just leave the past in the past, now? We both made mistakes. We've both been hurt. But there is no one else I want to be with, no one else I want to wake up next to, no one else I want to share my hopes and fears, and future, with than you. If you feel the same, don't we owe it to ourselves, and each other, to just… be happy?'

'Happy,' he repeated, like it hadn't really occurred to him. But then, slowly, a smile spread across his face, broad and genuine and so filled with hope that Annie's heart did thump almost out of her chest.

'Yes, happy,' she agreed, leaning forward, so her lips were just a hair's breadth from his. 'For as long as we both shall live.'

'Yes, my darling, my dearest, most beautiful Mrs Leonidas. For as long as we both shall live.'

Theo had not come to Sydney alone. He couldn't have, even if he'd wanted to. By that point, out of sheer necessity, he and Elliot Langley had become a unified force, focused solely on their shared need of finding Annie and knowing that she was safe.

When Theo got the call that Annie had been discovered, via a forgotten-about credit card, it was his private jet that had flown them halfway across the world. And locked in that plane together for twenty-four hours, Theo and Elliot had had very little option but to talk.

Theo had always found it hard to open up about his life, his childhood, and particularly with a man like Elliot, and yet, for Annie, he did so. He explained what his life had been like, why Elliot's insults had fundamentally changed him, had turned him so utterly bitter, had made him turn on Annie, too, to the point, and much to his shame, that when her mother died, he hadn't even reached out to her.

He'd been so angry, it was a miracle to think she'd found it in her heart to love him after that.

And yet she did, because she was Annie, full of light and love, full of compassion.

Elliot was an aristocrat to the core, and he found it hard to shake his views, but as he spoke about his daughter, who had died, and his and his late wife's hopes for Annie, Theo came to understand him better. To see that he'd been right about the older man. While his love for Annie was not as Theo would have wished, it was still love.

'I suppose even the royal family are allowed to marry commoners,' Elliot had conceded, as the plane came in over Sydney. And then, with a frown, as if he was reshaping his views of the world, bit by bit, 'Let's go find our girl, Theo.'

* * *

It was entirely surreal for Annie to be in Sydney, sitting beside her husband and opposite her father, over a high tea the following afternoon. Even stranger to hear her husband and father talk about the business, about the direction Theo was taking it in—and for Annie to see her father revitalised in those conversations, showing a genuine interest in the business for the first time in years.

By the time they finished tea, Annie felt almost as though she'd stepped into an alternate dimension—and she wasn't complaining.

They left Sydney the next morning, but almost as soon as touching down in Athens, and having Elliot disembark, Annie and Theo left once more, this time, returning to the island. Where their first trip there had been marked by long stretches of silence, this trip was the opposite. They talked the entire journey to the island, and once they arrived, instead of walking on eggshells, they were floating on air.

It was as though by finally accepting that he could love Annie, and accept that opening himself up to their relationship fully made him strong rather than weak, he stepped into a whole new reality. One in which he wanted her to understand everything about him, to know his entire truth, his childhood, the despair of it, because he was no longer grieving it—it was a part of him, and all those parts had led him to Annie, and the most all-consuming joy he could ever have imagined.

A year later, as they marked their first wedding anniversary, they were celebrating not only the fact that they'd found their way back to one another, but also the floating of the Langley company on the stock exchange as one of the highest offerings of all time, thanks to Theo's tireless efforts to turn it around. As for Annie, she was on the brink of opening her art gallery, and Theo was her biggest supporter and champion. His own achievements didn't get a look in: everything he said and did was about Annie, and how proud he was of her.

In its first year of operation, the gallery took the art world by storm, and though that brought Annie no small measure of joy, it was the discovery, three months after opening the doors, that their happy pairing was about to become a trio. Two years later, two more babies turned them into a five-person family, and five years after that, quite by surprise, another little Leonidas flew into their nest.

Though they loved and lived the rest of their lives in the fullness of those happy hearts, Annie and Theo devoted a lot of their time and money beyond their family, to street children. They raised money and awareness, built shelters, developed education programs, employment opportunities and therapy assistance.

From the wreckage of Theo's childhood had come something wonderful, and even as a very old man, Theo almost couldn't believe how rich and happy his life had become, all because he'd finally opened himself to love.

* * * * *

Get up to 4 Free Books!

**We'll send you 2 free books from each series you try
PLUS a free Mystery Gift.**

Both the **Harlequin Presents** and **Harlequin Medical Romance** series
feature exciting stories of passion and drama.